The Ties That Bind Us

EDEN EMORY

For those who prefer the flawed, ugly, messy emotions that live in us all.

The Ties That Bind Us

Cover design by eden emory

Edits by Lilly

ISBN 978-1-7376000-6-0 (paperback)

ISBN 978-1-7376000-2-2 (ebook)

www.ellemaebooks.com

Also By

Elle Mae:

Blood Bound Series:

Contract Bound: A Lesbian Vampire Romance

Lost Clause

Winterfell Academy Series:

The Price of Silence: Winterfell Academy Book 1

The Price of Silence: Winterfell Academy Book 2

The Price of Silence: Winterfell Academy Book 3

The Price of Silence: Winterfell Academy Book 4

The Price Of Silence: Winterfell Academy Book 5

Short and Smutty:

The Sweetest Sacrifice: An Erotic Demon Romance

Eden Emory:

The Ties That Bind Us

Don't Stop Me

Don't Leave Me

Don't Forget Me

Don't Hate Me

Hide N' Seek

Rate Race

Two of a Kind

Note

This is not your typical love story. This is a dark story with triggers such as dubious consent, cheating, orgasm denial/overload, mention of trafficking, domestic abuse, death, violence, and other sensitive topics.

If this does not interest you please close the book now.

For those who need resources:

National Suicide Prevention Lifeline
1-800-273-8255
https://suicidepreventionlifeline.org/

National Domestic Violence Hotline
1-800-799-7233
https://www.thehotline.org/

The Ties That Bind Us

EDEN EMORY

Jean

I have had to do many things in my life to make sure rent was paid and that I had food in my belly. A barista, an online English teacher, a freelance writer, hell I even worked on a farm part-time milking cows. Though truth be told, it wasn't all bad. Some jobs made some really good money and allowed me to keep my apartment for another month. Up until now, I have done everything and anything under the sun to earn a living because unlike many of the men I surround myself with, I wasn't born with a silver spoon in my mouth.

Mine instead was rusted and gnarled but I refused to let it be the death of me. My whole life I was adamant about not letting what I was born into define how my life was going to end. So, once I was finally of legal age and found a job that paid well, I went to the closest, cheapest college, paid for my degree with the money I earned, and even bought a nice apartment.

It was satisfying knowing that even though the work was hard, I could do this. I could make a living for myself and not have to rely on anyone else. But those times never lasted long, and here I was again—selling my soul for more money. Even after working and saving up for so long, money had been hard to come by recently and I was forced to fall back onto what I knew best: escorting.

It was my least favorite job that I had ever done.

I laughed as balding loser men told worn jokes to their bosses, family, or whomever else they needed to coddle up to all while they had no idea that I was paid help. They would parade me around like I was the newest shiniest toy, and I would have to act the part. They used this as a front so that people wouldn't start to question what they *really* did in their free time. While the secrets that they kept were always different, they were all keeping something. Something that would be glaringly obvious if they didn't have someone to distract the crowd with.

That's where I come in.

I don't just laugh at their jokes, or fan their ego. My job is much bigger than that. I work the crowds they bring me to make them *love* the idea of me. Have an uptight boss? I can act as the overly nice and secretly flirtatious girlfriend. Need help with public speaking? No one will look at you when I *accidentally* bend over to give those watching a look at what was underneath my incredibly short dress.

Sometimes the men that hire me are cute and more than once they were in the closet and used me as a way to get their parents off their back. But those jobs rarely lasted and are looked at like a diamond in the rough. The other girls and I would fight over them, trying to get away from the more notorious ones. Those ones always kept coming around and had proven to be a steady source of income, but were the least enjoyable. Those clients *hated* the idea of getting close to women and only saw us as maids and glorified sex toys. You were in trouble if one took a liking to you.

And by the looks of the man that had his arm wrapped around my shoulder, I was the one in trouble tonight.

When I first met Gary I thought I had gotten lucky. He wasn't unattractive per se...he just was socially awkward with women, or at least so I thought. As I got to know him, more socially awkward with women turned into severe mommy issues and a hatred for anything with a pussy between its legs.

The sides of his eyes creased as he smiled at his coworker in front of him. His pearly white teeth sparkled even under the dim light of the room. His salt and pepper hair had been combed back giving you a great look at his bright hazel eyes and full lips. His pale skin had a slight flush on his cheeks making him look younger than he really was. Anyone else would think the flush was from the alcohol or because of his hot date...but I knew better.

Lizzy, I think her name was, laughed along with us, her blond hair swinging wildly as she threw her head back. She would be pretty next to him too, a blonde-haired blue-eyed model type that would stand out of the crowd. Even now, I could see the wandering eyes in the room shift to her as she laughed. When she bid a goodbye I heard Gary let out a heavy sigh.

He hates these types of girls, I thought. *Girls that are better than him.*

I couldn't be one of those though, because he clearly knew what I did for a living and that alone made my presence bearable.

"Thanks for coming tonight," he spoke in a low tone and pushed me across the room—straight towards the alcohol. There wasn't a huge crowd, but people still moved out of the way as we walked as if they already knew whatever secret Gary was hiding and decided they didn't like it.

The event of the night was a small get-together for his work, but for people in his world a *small get-together* consisted of at least a hundred people lazily making small talk in one of their boss' mansions. It was a world I had never really belonged to but because of my job I got to understand more of what *really* happens here.

Many of the people that are invited are clueless and think that their boss is just showing off their luxurious mansion, one-of-a-kind paintings, and Michelin star chefs, but the reality was much darker. Behind closed doors there was money being shifted from one dirty hand to another, and you could bet that there was not a single clean person behind those doors. The sales and terms always differed but one of the most common among rich people were drugs and irregulated goods.

I never wanted to get caught in anything like that again, so I tried to leave these things as fast as possible.

Gary handed me a glass of bubbling liquid with a forced smile that looked more like a grimace than anything.

"Don't mention it," I said with a smile and took the champagne glass out of his hands. I took a sip and held his arm closer, pushing it against my front. I swore I saw the side of his mouth twitch. "Thanks for remembering me after three long years."

"Unfortunately, there are some people who would probably remember you," he said with a sigh and looked over at the couple who were talking in hushed tones near an intricate panting of two women in a *very sexual* act.

I felt a smile tug at my lips when I realized how uncomfortable he must be in this house. During the time we first met he made damn sure that I knew what was and was not acceptable in his eyes. After all, I would have to know if I were to pose as his girlfriend, right?

PDA, women's empowerment, sex work, and pro-choice were all things he loathed to talk about. He made it very clear that the only reason he hired me was to be a means to an end and he would hate every moment that I touched him.

I hummed, my eyes unable to move from the painting. It was beautiful. Two women together, one laid out on a bed with the other woman's head buried between her legs. Even though the girl's red hair sprawled out wildly around her, there was no hiding the *very detailed* pussy that glared back at us.

"Very unfortunate," I murmured. "That you haven't gotten a real girlfriend during that time."

I peeked over and watched Gary's face redden further. I let out a giggle and forced an easygoing smile to my face. Some people looked over and when they did I looped my fingers through Gary's belt loop.

It was more than he liked, but I was having fun in the moment and feeling the effects of alcohol.

"And that you haven't learned how to respect yourself in that time," he shot back.

I let out another loud giggle to annoy him.

"What is the occasion?" I asked in an excited whisper and took another sip of my champagne before giving the frozen man some space. I watched as a couple walked past us. The man was dressed in a full suit while the woman wore a loose-fitting short dress that draped around her body more similar to a bed sheet than a piece of clothing. The blood-red color of her dress brought out the beautiful hues of her skin making her look like a walking Calla lily.

Her brown eyes met mine and she gave me a wink. It was my turn to flush under her attention and I couldn't help but feel self-conscious when I was next to someone so regal. She wasn't the only one though, many people here were dressed in outfits that had been perfectly tailored to them, clothes that I could never dream to afford.

I had to ask Caroline for the fitted black dress that I had on right now because there was no way I would be able to afford one. She had of course given me her most expensive one and wished me good luck with a wink as she literally pushed me out of her door. She was the person in charge of the escorting agency and had been running it for as long as I have known her. She was a vicious little lady that loved to bleed money out of rich men, hence the business she started. I did not know the cut she took out of this, but I know between me and her fifteen other girls, she was able to afford a penthouse right in Manhattan. She was the one who so graciously called me back after a three-year break promising two grand for the night, and of course I couldn't say no to that.

Imagine my surprise when I saw one of my least favorite clients at her side after so many years.

"For everyone else, there is none," Gary said. "For me though,

I get to meet someone very important tonight." His Adam's apple bobbed as he swallowed.

"Congratulations are in order," I said playfully making sure to show my teeth as I smiled. Everything is about looks in this job, that's why I was in a salon chair for hours today. He had specifically requested my hair to be in modest waves and my makeup to be natural as possible, which took much longer than you would think, even with multiple people fussing over me.

"I guess." He tried to act nonchalant, but I heard the bit of pride seep through his voice. "I don't have to remind you not to speak of this outside these walls."

"Contracts, NDAs, privacy policies, all remind me on your behalf," I said with a wink.

He let out a grunt of acknowledgment and nothing more before looking at his watch.

"Let's go," he said and grabbed my drink from me only to discard it on an empty table as we walked toward the back of the house. The people around us were laughing, getting drunk, and just enjoying their lives so they didn't even blink as we pushed past them. Their carefree attitudes should have made me feel better, but I still had to wipe my sweaty palms on my dress and it didn't stop my heart from racing wildly.

This wasn't the first time I had been in a situation like this. With my *many* odd jobs came many odd and even dangerous situations. I was supposed to be protected by aliases and contracts but those could only go so far.

Gary led me through two crowded rooms and the music finally started to fade as we walked down a long hallway. I spotted a door with two burly-looking men beside it; both of their heads turned to watch us approach. The bald one with an angry face gave me a once-over while the one with a buzz cut glared at Gary.

"Gary Walters," he said. "And my date Marissa."

I gave them my prettiest little smile and sent them a small wave, trying not to show how much my body was pushing me to run back to safety. There were only a few reasons why a door would need to be guarded and I really didn't want to find out why. The bald guy looked us over once, twice, then huffed and opened the door for us.

Inside was a cozy room with bookshelves for walls, a fireplace that was currently lit, and two loveseats that sat right in the middle of the room with a table in between them. Small, intimate, and definitely unescapable. There wasn't even a window. There was a man standing towards the fireplace with his back turned towards us, who turned only after the door behind us shut with a soft click. With a shock, I realized that I recognized him.

"Marissa?" Jonathan asked, his dark eyes going round in surprise. He had aged much over the last three years, his hair almost entirely grey and the wrinkles on his forehead more prominent. His once tanned skin seemed to have faded. He was a sweet guy, who was very attentive when I was around, but I knew that his eyes were far too sharp to *just* be a finance guy like he claimed to be.

I guess I finally got to see the business he is in.

"Jonathan!" I exclaimed softly and left Gary's side to walk into his open arms. "So nice to see you. So sorry I haven't been able to make it to your last get-together."

"Oh no need to fret, dear," Jonathan said and pulled back to look at me at arm's length, much like a grandparent would. "Gary let us know about your family. My condolences."

I swallowed thickly not even having to fake this quiver in my bottom lip. I really wished Gary had used any other excuse but no, apparently multiple deaths in the family had to be the reason for his escort to go missing.

"Thank you," I said sincerely. "I'm just happy Gary was there with me through it all, such a sweet man." I looked over to Gary to give him a small smile. He tried and failed to send me one back.

When Jonathan finally unhanded me I walked over to Gary's side. I now understood why he wanted me specifically to come tonight. Jonathan had a sweet spot for me and sought me out every time I was with Gary for the night. Of course he would ask about me, and this was most likely an attempt to butter him up.

"You can sit if you'd like," Jonathan said and poured himself a whiskey from the bar cart to our left. "But the guest of honor will be here soon."

He poured me one as well and sent me a knowing smile. I took the glass; over the few times I had seen him he had caught on far too quickly to my drinking habits... It was just about the only real thing he knew about me. The only thing I let slip.

"We have partnered with her to help take care of her business' finances," he explained. "Quite a big investment with lots of money moving around at once. It took a long to steal her from *Christian's* company, but I finally got her for a night and I am introducing her to our best."

The way he spit "Christian" out made my stomach flip. I looked over to gauge Gary's reaction to the news. Any other man would have been swelling with pride at the thought of working with such a highly sought out client, but there was one flaw in Jonathan's plan.

"A girl?" he asked seemingly unable to help himself.

Jonathan sent me a look full of pity as if I actually had to deal with the guy that had a firm grip on my waist.

"Yes," he answered. "And may I remind you, a big investor."

The door behind us opened and we all turned to see who this mysterious investor was. My heart had been pounding so hard up until now that I had heard it in my ears, but when I saw the pitch-black hair and dark eyes of the person who peeked around the door my heart stopped completely and I felt an eerie silence fall around us.

The girl was unfazed as her hungry dark eyes drank in my form. The right side of her lip tugged into a smile, and I could see her sharp canines poke out. She was wearing an open chested black button-up that was dangerously close to showing the swell of her breast and a pair of blood-red slacks paired with black dress shoes.

Shae, my mind whispered panicked but also hungry, ready for her. This was worse than any other deal I could have imagined. I would rather be stuck in this room with crates of drugs than have to breathe the same air as her. The windowless room seemed even smaller now and my mind went into overdrive. I would need to get out of here while not totally blowing my cover.

She was the ex of nightmares. Our relationship had been an intoxicating one that made adrenaline pump through my veins and my mouth water even just thinking of it. This was the girl that had haunted every dark corner, every wet dream, and had this vice-like grip on my life for the last three years while I fought off the heartbreak of what happened between us. She was the sole reason why I was in the position that I was in now, groveling like a dog for every penny I could get. If she would have just been a decent human being I wouldn't have struggled as hard the last three years without her.

I hated her as much as I wanted her.

Her ringed fingers ran through her short hair, and I swear I saw an evil glint pass her eyes as she made contact with mine. It was far too easy to remember what those eyes looked like as she hovered over me in the middle of the night, too easy to remember how sure and confident those hands were as they roamed my thighs, and far too easy to get lost in the way her breath felt against my sweaty skin. A shock went through me when I was brought back to reality by Jonathan's excited tone.

"Shae, please meet Gary and his girlfriend Marissa. Gary has recently been promoted and will be taking over your accounts," he said and shook her hand enthusiastically but did not pull her into a hug like he did with me. If she was here, he should know just what type of illegal shit she was into.

"Marissa, is it?" Her voice vibrated through me and even after all these years I felt my knees go weak. I swallowed thickly and tried to put on my acting face while her eyes pierced through me.

"Yes it is," I said sweetly. "I am just here to say hello to

Jonathan here. I can leave so you three can continue with your business."

I readied myself to leave but she gave me a shit-eating grin and waved me off instead.

"No need," she said looking me up and down. "You can act as our drink girl. That seems like a fitting job for someone of *your status.*"

Heat flared in me, this time from anger as she took my glass of whiskey out of my hands and stared at me as she threw back the entire thing. Gary and Jonathan watched in a tense silence, probably wondering just how far this would go. I just knew Gary was trying to piece together what exactly was happening.

Her eyes seemed to dare me to say something, dare me to push back. I wouldn't have been so pissed if it was anyone else, but she had known how much I hated being degraded like that in front of these people. I may have had to work jobs that others would think were unsightly, but I was still a human and deserved to be treated with respect.

She pushed the empty glass back into my hands and shot Gary a smile before moving to sit in the chair. She spread her legs wide and shifted in the chair all eyeing me while she did so, as if to prove that she was in charge and unforgettable.

You are in trouble, her gaze seemed to say. *You are going to wish you never left me.*

The tension between us flitted through the air and I felt a prickle on the back of my neck. Gary and Jonathan had no idea that the flood gates of bad history had just broken open and now was just the calm before the storm. In the three years since I left she had not changed one bit, and it only assured me that no matter how attractive, rich, or powerful she was, that I had taken the right course.

"Let's get started shall we?" she said with a smugness in her tone. "And pour the men another one would you, love?"

With gritted teeth I did as she asked. If I messed up now there was no way I would be getting paid for tonight, and that was the most important thing. As long as I could get the money, and get out of here without a scratch, I would swallow my pride and serve her. As I turned and walked towards the cart I could feel her gaze as if it was physically burning into me. It was different from the men; it felt like she was claiming me, and I could feel the heat rush across my skin.

When I turned back I saw Shae's fingers trail across her lips. I licked my own without thinking. With a shaky breath I prepared myself and walked back to her side. She looked up at me as I came closer to her but her eyes stopped short, right at my breasts.

I didn't let it annoy me; I know she was doing this on purpose. She wanted to see me break, mess up. It was all a game for her, it always had been, and I was just a toy she liked to play with. I placed the glass on the table beside her and gave her a wide smile before turning back to Gary and Jonathan.

"Marissa, Kathy has been dying to see you," Jonathan said in a cheerful tone. "Why don't you go find her. I'm sure we won't take long here and then you and Gary can be on your lovely way."

I smiled at him, a real one this time, thankful to get out of here.

Shae didn't say anything as I left, and I made sure to make a show of kissing Gary right on the lips before leaving. I normally wouldn't have, I have a strict no intimacy policy with clients and he fucking hates me, but I wanted to piss Shae off as much as she was pissing me off.

Two could play at that game, I thought and looked back at her as my hand wrapped around the cool metal door handle. I wanted to scream the words but instead I settled for a sickly-sweet smile. *You don't own me anymore.*

I ran out of the room as fast as I could without looking too idiotic. I did not look back at the guards or anyone as I speed walked to one of the many single powder rooms the mansion had. I locked the door behind me and bolted to the sink before turning on the faucet and splashing cool water on my neck.

"Jesus fuck," I hissed as I looked at my flushed face in the mirror. My normally cream cheeks had a bright red color to them that was definitely not makeup, and it went all the way to my ears and down my neck. My knees were still shaking, and I placed my hand over my chest feeling my erratically beating heart.

How the fuck did this happen? I thought to myself, panicked.

The first night I had come back to escorting just *had to* be the same night that I would run into my ex after three years. I had moved on, or at least I thought I had. Seeing her stupid smirk and heated eyes seemed to violently throw me back into the place I was three years prior. A lost hopeless child who was in way over their head and happily losing themselves in the most dangerous person they could find.

Shae was dangerous in more ways than one. She had a sharp tongue and explosive temper, but she was also New York's best and most ruthless art dealer. While normal art dealers had a somewhat legal occupation, Shae thrived on the business in the underworld. She was the one that showed me that I didn't belong in this world. She showed me just how dangerous they could be, but I was so lost back then that I *actually liked* the danger. I craved it.

Craved *her*.

I splashed water on my neck one more time, taking a deep breath. Then another. Then another.

When I looked up again the redness had dramatically decreased, and I was left staring back at my own wide brown eyes. Those same eyes had seen the rise and fall of our relationship and I couldn't help but see how tired they have become compared to just three short years ago. I jumped when there was a knock at the door.

"Occupied," I called and carefully readjusted my dress. It was a bit too short on me and had risen as I was fleeing from that room. That was no look for my role tonight, I had to be better. Look at least somewhat put together or else the vultures would descend on me and Gary, and that would not do well for my paycheck.

The knock came again, and I let out a frustrated sigh before steeling myself. I walked to the door and swung it open, only to wish I hadn't.

Shae stood there, her arm against the door frame and a smirk on her face. Those eyes narrowed on me, and my skin became unbearably hot. I took a startled step back and she used that to push into the powder room and lock the door behind her.

"Don't," I warned but my voice lost its strength as she took a step towards me.

"Don't what *Marissa?*" Her tone was mocking. I took a step back and she took one forward pushing me further into the room. Her spicy cologne filled my senses, and a shuddering breath left my lips.

"I should be out there," I said and moved to step around her, but she stepped to the side blocking my path.

This time when I stepped back my backside hit the edge of the sink. She leaned forward, putting both hands on either side of me and leaned forward so our bodies were centimeters away from each other. I could feel her hot breath waft across my face; it still smelt like whiskey.

This was *dangerous.* I had never planned to be in this situation ever again and I knew that with one wrong move I would be spiraling down into Shae once more. I didn't want to play this with her. I wanted to forget her and move on. Live a happy, peaceful, easy life. Something she could never give me.

"What gives you the audacity to think you can just run away again, hm?" she asked dangerously. "Are you really that stupid? Do you really think I wasn't about to come in here and remind you exactly what you have been missing all these years?"

"Shae, we broke up," I said trying to muster anger in my tone, but it sounded weak, breathy almost.

Her eyes flashed and in a moment she closed the space between us, pushing me into the counter with one hand against my neck the other tugging at my hair.

Dangerous indeed.

Shae

I have never in my life met someone as infuriating as the goddess under me right now. I had waited, bided my time for *three long years* until she finally got the sense to return.

I let her have her little meltdown. Let her do—God only knows what, but I had promised myself that as soon as she crossed my path again I would get her back for leaving me high and dry with no warning whatsoever.

I knew we would cross each other's path at one point and if there was anything my job had taught me, patience was by far the thing I had the most of. But seeing her with that sad sack of a man was my final straw. I had thought that after all those years that I could do this right, *better* than before...but I couldn't help myself.

Once more I found myself being pushed to the limits by her, acting in ways I would never do to another.

"You really think we broke up?" I asked her in a growl. "That's funny."

I ground my hips into her, and her hand flew up to my chest, trying to push me away. I only tightened my grip on her hair and forced her head back even further. She let out a low groan that ignited a feral feeling inside me. I wanted to lash out at her, make her beg to be released. Only then would I know that I would own her fully.

I wanted to get back at her so bad. The dull aching wound in my chest from her leaving seemed to open up with her being so close and I felt just like I did back then.

But you are different now, a voice said in my head, though I doubted its authenticity.

"I left you," she choked out between those perfectly pink lips. God I missed this so much, missed the way they felt in the morning when she woke me up. Missed when she would bite down on her bottom lip as she tried to keep her moans sealed inside her. She tried to act innocent, like this wasn't what she wanted...but I *knew her* better than that.

I looked down at her tight-fitting dress that was already pushed up to her mid-thigh. I forced my leg between her legs, kicking her feet apart and pushed my knee into her core. She could fight me if she really wanted to but instead her hands tightened around my shirt and pulled me closer.

I leaned down and nipped at her bottom lip, loving the way her eyes widened at my actions.

"I *let you* leave," I told her. "And now I am here to take you back."

I heard her suck in an air of breath. I licked her bottom lip teasingly slow; I could taste the sweetness of her and it almost sent me into a ravenous rage. I had been patient, but even that was wearing thin. I had not been with a person since she left, and I could only think about bending her over and fucking her against this counter until she screamed.

"I'm here with someone," she said quickly, *too quickly.*

"Yes, Marissa. I know," I said teasingly. "He won't miss you and I made sure that he would give you a *very nice tip* tonight."

I would never work with him in a million years if it wasn't for her. I had come here with the full intention to turn him down after doing my *research,* but she threw a wrench in that.

I wound my arm around her waist and forced her down on

my knee harshly. She let out a strangled moan. It wasn't long before I felt the first rock of her hips against me and the heat of her core seep through my pants. Warmth coiled in my own belly as I watch her flush. I smirked at her and unwound my fingers from her silky hair to grab a hold of her hips helping her grind against my knee.

"See?" I asked her and leaned closer to almost kiss her, but pulled away just as her face tilted up to mine. "You're already bending so quickly. Let's not kid ourselves."

"Why are you doing this?" she asked in a breathy voice before letting out a small moan as I pushed my knee harder into her. I wanted her aching tomorrow, remembering the way it felt to ride me.

"I told you," I hissed. "I'm here to bring you back, now bend over like a good girl and let me fuck your brains out, then we can go on our way."

Whatever I said must have snapped her out of it because in an instant the breathy moaning goddess under me turned into an angry cat I had messed with too many times. I had seen this look before. With the strength I knew she was hiding she pushed me off her and I stumbled back trying to catch myself.

"And I told you *three years ago,*" she hissed. "Stay the fuck out of my life."

I ground my teeth feeling anger rise up in me fast. She turned on her heels and stomped towards the door.

"You better think twice about that," I called to her. "If you come back now, I'll go easy on you."

No one, and I mean *no one* in all my years of business had crossed me. They didn't dare. But she never seemed to have the same fear as them. No matter how many times I had shown her, she always came back with that same attitude.

It infuriated me as much as it excited me.

She sent me a glare over her shoulder that only caused my core to clench. I fucking loved it when she gave me that look.

"Go find someone else's life to ruin," she hissed at me and left the powder room without another word.

I let out a chuckle, as my anger festered into something else. Without waiting another second, I picked up my phone and dialed a number I had kept for longer than four years.

My least favorite person picked up on the second ring.

"Don't even think about it," came Caroline's southern drawl from the other line.

"So, you still kept my number after all this time," I said with a teasing tone. "I didn't know you missed me so much."

She let out a loud mocking laugh from the other end. I felt a smile play at my lips. As annoying as she could be...she used to be fun. At least she was when she wasn't pimping out escorts left and right. Back when she was still a young college woman, with more money than she ever needed happily gifted from her various sugar daddies.

"Even if the next time I see you is when we are in hell, I would say that's far too soon," she spat at me.

"I'm too pure for hell," I teased. "You on the other hand..."

"I am hangin' up," she huffed.

"Wait," I rushed out. "Five grand."

As sure as I was that night would be dark, I was surer about Caroline being money hungry.

"I'm not doing it," she hissed.

"I didn't even ask yet," I said.

The door to the powder room opened showing a very drunk couple. Their clothes were halfway off by the time they noticed that I was standing there. I rolled my eyes and left the room only to hear them locking the door right behind me.

"I know what you want," she said in an accusing tone. "And I would be a shit friend if I did that to her."

"Ten grand," I said as Gary and Jonathan stepped out of the room I left them in. I watched as Jean smiled that stupid fake smile at him and wrapped her arm around his waist. I knew it was escort business, but it still made my chest heavy with jealousy.

Caroline cursed on the other line.

The others still hadn't noticed me yet, and I watched as Gary's hand rested on Jean's hip. It was far too close to her ass for my liking and on cue I felt my mouth curl into a scowl.

"Twelve," I pushed not willing to wait any longer. "You take nine, give her three. She doesn't have to know."

I knew Caroline was foaming at the mouth at the thought of all that money. I was silently begging her to take it as I watched Jean bark out a fake laugh that caused heads to turn to her. She was beautiful, anyone could see that, but no one knew the *real* her. *That* was saved just for me and I reveled in that fact.

"She's going to hate me," Caroline whispered.

"She will get over it," I hissed at her. "Do we have a deal or not?"

"God damnit, Shae. We have a deal. I better see that money in my bank account tomorrow morning," she growled.

I let out a laugh.

"It'll be under that shitty Honda of yours in twenty. Get me a Friday night," I said and hung up without another word.

They all turned to me as I walked up to them. I didn't give a shit about Gary and Jonathan and locked my eyes with Jean only before running my eyes down the length of her body. I watched in sweet satisfaction as she pushed her thighs together. I knew she was wet under there, aching. God she was so perfect, so receptive, and still all mine.

I couldn't wait to surprise her.

THREE YEARS EARLIER

Caroline had a firm grip on my hand as she weaved us through the impressive amount of people packed into this penthouse. It was by no means a small place, but the amount of people here was insane. There was barely enough room to stand without brushing elbows with someone.

I gripped my purse tightly feeling the effects of the drinking from earlier wash over me. We had partied before this and I was ready to call it a night, but when Caroline had gotten a call she insisted that we drop everything and rush over to this place. Even with the people packed in it I could see how meticulously the space was taken care of. The marble floors were spotless and there was not a piece of trash in sight even as some of the people around us got rowdy.

The thing that took my breath away though, was the art that decorated the place. On every other wall there were intricate paintings that looked like so much more than your average IKEA painting and they each held a distinct aura to them that kept drawing my attention. My fuzzy brain sought out a shiny emerald one that called to me from across the room and I couldn't think of anything else as Caroline stopped at the home bar that was tucked away near the living room.

The painting seemed to be baiting me as we pushed through the crowd of people, begging me to pay attention to it. It could have been the booze or something else entirely, but I felt as though it would be a loss if I did not go over and take a peek at it.

Caroline smiled sweetly at one of the three bartenders that were attending the people around us and began spouting out words in her sweet southern accent, no doubt trying to sway over the bartenders in hopes that they would continue to serve two already drunk women. I didn't even pay attention to what she ordered until it was pushed into my hand. I looked over to her to protest but was not surprised to see my side now empty.

Caroline had the tendency to do that when she got excited. She, like myself, was drawn to the newest and fanciest thing that she could find. Though she was much more extroverted than me and willing to actually go out there and get it, while I would stay in the corner.

Sometimes I would take just an ounce of the courage that she was exuding and put myself out there, but that was not for tonight. Instead, I focused on blending back into the crowd, ignoring the chattering around me.

My eyes were drawn back to the painting right by the entrance that spanned almost the entire back wall. Without commanding my feet to move, I found myself gravitating towards it as if the pull that I imagined was real.

The closer I got the easier it was to see that the painting was three-dimensional and stuck out in odd ways. I cocked my head to get a better look at the intricacies of it. It was the most beautiful piece I had ever seen and it took my breath away. To think that an artist had the mind to create something like this. It made me remember my own failed attempts in high school art class. While I loved the *idea* of being an artist I never found much success in the implementation of it.

I stepped back to get a better look, whispering an apology to whomever I bumped into but didn't bother to look at their face. I was too drunk to *actually* care what others thought of me and was slowly shrugging off my introverted tendencies. When I was sober it would have affected me way more, but now I just wanted to stare at the art.

Taking a sip of my drink I grimaced when fuzzy sweetness exploded on my tongue. I glared down at the drink, angry that it pulled me out of the wonder of the art before me. A chuckle sounded from my right.

When I looked over to see who it was my breath caught in my throat.

I was no stranger to attractive people. Hell, because of my job I saw them all the time. Not the clients so much as the people they surrounded themselves with, but it was all the same. *She* was different though.

She wore a suit jacket that lay open exposing the sliver of skin all the way from the hollow of her throat to right above her navel where her pants were buckled. The dark black fabric made her stand out among the sea of people that wore emerald, white, and red. It was an effort to drag my eyes away from where I could see the slight swell of her breast and to her eyes. They were almost as dark as her suit and were currently locked onto me. Her dark hair was slicked back showing her undercut and I wanted badly to run my hands through her hair.

Her pink plump lips quirked into a smirk when she noticed my staring.

God she was fucking beautiful.

I wanted this girl to destroy my life and laugh in my face as I cried.

"I didn't know my sense of art was so distasteful," she said in a tone that almost sounded teasing.

I could feel my face heat and I panicked to find the words.

"No-o, it's just the drink is not my thing. My friend sh—"

"I'm kidding," she said and reached for my drink. I jumped when her fingers brushed across mine as she gently took the drink from my hand. Her other hand pushed a short glass into my hand,

and I could smell the whiskey coming from it. "You look like a whiskey person."

I am now, I thought in my head. If this girl wanted me to be a whiskey person, vodka person, I would do it.

Her smile didn't fade as she took a big swig of the drink in her hand. I watched in fascination at the movement in her throat as she did so.

"*Jesus,*" I mumbled. Her widening eyes told me I had said that a bit *too* loud. I swallowed thickly and took a sip of the whiskey she had handed me. It took almost everything I had not to grimace when the taste hit my tongue.

"Shae actually," she said with a glint in her eyes.

"What?" I sputtered. I rubbed my slick palms against my dress. The room felt too hot and my dress too tight.

"My name," she explained. "Is Shae, not Jesus."
Fucking hell.

"Jean," I said and tried to coolly look back at the art in front of us. Maybe I still had a chance to redeem myself. "I actually like the colors a lot."

Shae hummed next to me, and I felt her shift, her arm brushing against mine. The touch set my heart racing. I was tempted to shift away because her presence was just too much, even as she stewed in the silence between us I could feel her confidence radiate out of her.

I was dying to know what she was thinking.

The silence was starting to feel uncomfortable, and I swear I could feel her eyes burning into me.

"I don't know much about art—" I cut off mid-sentence when I turned to look up at her only to realize she was already leaning towards me. Her face was mere inches from mine, and I could smell the alcohol coming out of her parted lips.

I tried not to let my gaze wander to where her jacket hung, giving me an unobstructed view of her breasts and erect nipples but I couldn't help myself. My mouth watered at the sight, and I yearned to taste one.

"Want to fuck in the bathroom?" she asked. Her hand came up to cup my heated face and her thumb traced my lower lip. I shivered at the action.

"*Yes please*," I said, my voice barely above a whisper.

She straightened with a small chuckle and threw an arm around my shoulder.

"I can't wait to hear you beg," she said in a dark voice.

I didn't know how detrimental this night would have been to my entire life but still to this day, I do not regret saying yes to her in that moment.

Gary indeed gave me a huge tip that night. Almost a whole grand. Apparently Shae was so happy with *Marissa* that she signed the contract right after I left the room.

When I entered my dark apartment I could still feel my core fluttering with the feeling of Shae's knee as she forced me to grind against her. I had let it go on too far and now that I was in the safety of my own home and not surrounded by the madness that was Shae... I began to feel guilty.

I took my shoes off slowly and placed my bag on the counter, making sure to hide the money in the small vase I kept right by the door. I wouldn't be able to explain the money if I was asked so I thought to hide it now would be best.

It was a short walk to my bedroom and with each step, my resolve got weaker. While I was feeling an overwhelming amount of guilt, it didn't stop the ache in my core and there was no way I would be able to sleep at this rate if I didn't solve this problem.

"Jean?" came Hunter's sleep-filled voice from somewhere buried under the mountains of pillows and blankets that we kept on our bed. "Did you have a good time with Caroline?

"I did," I said in a sweet voice and reached around to undo my dress, letting it fall off me with ease.

Hunter was the only man I had ever dated and would be the last. Or at least I thought he would have been. After Shae, I vowed to never date again. I was ready to never have another relationship again until Hunter came along almost a year ago, the complete opposite of Shae.

First of all, he was obviously a guy. I had never been with one, so he opened an opportunity to experiment in a way I had never been able to. That was exciting to me and after a few times I figured that I quite liked being with a guy.

Second, he was the sweetest guy you could ever meet and was comparable to a puppy. Excited over everything and just happy to live his life. It was refreshing when I couldn't get out of my depression after everything had happened.

Third, he was an *honest good kid.* He grew up in a loving family, went to church, and worked for his father's company. Family was at the forefront of his mind and everything he did was selfless.

I snuck into the bed and pushed back the covers. Hunter was barely awake; I could hear his deep breaths and his eyes barely opened as the bed dipped beside him.

"I'm glad, babe," he whispered. "Come to sleep, it's late."

Instead of letting him grab me I threw my leg over his hips and lowered myself onto him. He liked to sleep with no shirt on and in just a pair of boxer shorts so this would be easy.

He sucked in a harsh breath and his large hands flew up to my hips, locking me in place. I placed my hands on his broad chest and rocked into him. It wasn't long before he was hard, and I could hear soft moans tumble out of his lips.

Too easy, I thought almost in disappointment.

I leaned forward to kiss him, running my hands through his blond curly hair as I did so. I didn't think about how unsatisfying it was when his tongue invaded my mouth and how I wished that when his hands came up to push me closer that he would instead pull my hair and fuck me without mercy.

I sat up and unhooked my bra throwing it across the room. His fingers found my nipples almost immediately and began twisting them. When I gasped he sat up as well to bring one of my nipples into his mouth, and surprised me by biting on one.

"Yes," I moaned and arched into him. He froze for a split second before moving to bite on the other one. "I need you."

He let out a groan.

"Let me get a—"

"It's okay," I cut him off by pushing myself up just enough to bring his hard dick out. He resumed sucking on my nipples.

Unable to wait I pulled my panties aside and lowered myself onto him. I let out a loud moan as he slid into me. We both gasped when he thrust up into me and I began to rock, trying to still chase the feeling of euphoria Shae had pulled from me.

"Oh god, Jean," he moaned. "You feel so good."

I arched into him, bringing his mouth back to my nipples. He tried to set the pace, but it was too slow for me. Getting frustrated I pushed him back into the bed and rode him faster, pleasure finally shooting through me. It wasn't easy to imagine him being someone else when those groans kept coming out of his mouth.

Yes Jean.

You're so perfect.

Oh god.

His hands found my hips and now with each movement he thrust into me. I moaned loudly when he hit a spot that caused my body to go taut.

"Yes, like that," I said and kept my pace. I threw my head back and rode him even harder, the slaps of skin filling the room. I was so close I could feel the wave of heat build up, just waiting to be forced out. My pleasure was interrupted by a loud groan and before I could even prepare myself I felt his hot seed fill me.

Swallowing my disappointment, I pulled him out of me and rolled over onto my side of the bed.

Hunter turned and pulled me close to him.

"What got into you?" he whispered and gave me a small kiss behind my ear.

I tried hard to swallow my arousal, but I couldn't stop the images of Shae earlier this evening from infiltrating my mind. The way her hand felt around my throat when she had me at her mercy. The way my body positively lit up when she had whispered in my ear. Just thinking about it caused my core to clench.

She had almost made me come by riding her *fucking knee* and Hunter had only been able to make me come twice in the last year. I didn't answer but Hunter didn't seem to care because I heard his snores not a minute later. It was easy to push him off me and take myself to the bathroom.

Even as I stood under the hot water of the shower Shae was not far from my thoughts and I found myself finishing her job from earlier. As I rubbed my pulsing clit I thought of the heated gaze she gave me, the way her ringed fingers felt against my throat, how they grabbed my hair and commanded me to obey her.

I shuddered as I imagined her in the shower with me, whispering in my ear.

Good girl, she'd say. *That's right, imagine it's me that's finger fucking you right now. I knew you couldn't stay away.*

She would lick the length of my neck and then when she got tired of my pace—like she always would—she would take matters into her own hands.

I should have known you couldn't do the job, she'd hiss. *After all, it was meant for me.*

I came to the thought of her reaching around me to sink her fingers into my wet folds.

"This is fucked," I whispered.

❧

I WAS awoken by the sound of clanging pots and sizzling.

I laid in bed for a few minutes trying to wrap my head around what had happened last night. I still couldn't believe that after all these years she still looked and acted as if time had never passed. I had dreamt about when I'd see her again, and this time I had a plan.

If I ever saw her again I was sure to show her that I was happier, better off without her. That all of those awful things she said to me the night I left didn't matter anymore. I would look at her with a smile before turning away and never seeing her again... She would hate that.

Sometimes I fantasied about yelling at her until my throat was sore and my voice went out. I had never gotten that far with her; she always knew just how to shut me up and when all was said and done I would never have the energy to yell at her.

What worried me the most though was how adamant she was that we were still together. It should anger me...and I did have a tiny flame inside me burning at her audacity, but I knew her too well. When she promised something she would make sure it happened and last night didn't seem like a joke.

I heard Hunter turn off the stove and a wave of nausea hit my stomach. He didn't deserve this. I should march right in there and let him know exactly what went on last night...but then I would have to come clean about two things.

My escorting business. Which I had an inkling he would *really* not like.

And the fact that I was not straight and almost fucked my ex-girlfriend last night in a powder room all while being at a party for very illegal things.

Before I could stew in my guilt Hunter's flushed boyish face peeked around the door to our bedroom. He gave me a dazzling smile that showed his dimples.

"I made French toast," he said in an excited tone before coming fully into the room and walking towards our bed. Like I normally would, I peeled back the covers and opened my arms for him. With another smile he climbed back into the bed with me and wrapped his arms around my form. He smelled of sweet syrup.

"What's the occasion?" I asked and left a kiss on his chin, his stubble making my nose itch.

He inhaled deeply and left a kiss on my hair.

"I just want to take my girlfriend out to town, show her off a bit," he said in a light tone. "Or are you too hungover?"

I pulled away to give him a forced smile.

"I barely drank," I confessed.

He had a playful look on his face.

"Then what happened last night?" he asked, his hand gripping my hips and pulling me closer to him.

"I just missed you is all," I said and leaned in to give him a real kiss. When he deepened it I tried to allow myself to get lost in it, like I normally would, but the feelings of guilt held me back. But that was not all that held me back... All of a sudden his touches were wrong. The way his hand trailed up my waist, the way his knees forced my legs apart.

"Let's go eat," he said in a low tone. "If we start this now I'm afraid we will never get out of here."

I swallowed thickly and nodded at his lie. He was a good man, sometimes too good and in this case it meant that the sex was lacking. He was always stuck in the same routine. In the bedroom, with all of the lights off, lasting less than five minutes. It had taken me months to convince him to let me on top so at least I could control how hard I wanted it, but I still haven't been able to convince him to try doggy style. Last night was probably the kinkiest we have ever gotten before...and this was my sex life now. So, when I said that Hunter was the opposite of Shae...I meant it in every single way possible.

I tried not to get lost again in the thoughts of how Shae had once treated me. She was a shitty person but *God* did she know how to use her hands.

I let him drag me to the kitchen where our delicious-looking breakfast awaited us. I sat down with him at the bar and gave him a small smile before I dug into the toast.

"Jesus Hunter this is so good," I moaned around the food. He had always been a great cook; he cites the culinary classes he had taken in college but there had to be more than that. Every meal he made felt special. I wondered if he would ever consider giving up his father's company for a life as a chef, but threw the idea out of my mind.

He valued his father far too much for that.

"I used a bit of honey this time, do you taste it?" he asked and took a big bite out of his own French toast, almost completely devouring it in one bite.

"Yes, it's delicious," I said with a hum. "So where are we going today?"

He took a sip of water before answering, his eyes twinkling with mischief. I only just realized that he was still shirtless and wearing his boxers. Boxers that had stains from our late-night moment.

"It's a surprise," he said teasingly and finished his breakfast with one last bite before leaving his plate on the counter and standing to give me a kiss on the lips. "If you hurry I'll get you coffee from your favorite place."

He left me to go get ready in our room and I tried to finish as much of my breakfast as possible before he finished getting ready. Coffee was enough of a benefit for me, but my stomach was still feeling painfully nauseous.

I will need to come clean soon, about all of it.

The escorting.

The lesbian ex-girlfriend.

The debt.

He had to know because I had a sinking feeling that I knew what all this was leading up to. Our year anniversary was coming up and he had always mentioned taking things further after a year...or at least we would have a discussion around it. I didn't want to break up with him, but I sure as hell wasn't ready for whatever else he had in store for me.

There was a time where I had wanted more, wanted it all...but that was with the same person I was trying not to think about.

"Pull yourself together," I hissed as I angrily threw away the rest of the French toast. It plopped into the trash with a soggy slap that made my throat tighten.

Enough is enough.

WITH A FRESH LATTE IN HAND, Hunter led me through a very colorful and pleasant-smelling garden. It had taken us forty minutes to get here by car and I had no idea where we were. When we pulled up I got a look at a very expensive-looking house and assumed we were going inside, but instead Hunter sent me a smile and led me around the back, to a beautiful garden that seemed to span on for acres.

I never even knew some place like this was available in New York. Well, we were outside of the city but still... New York is expensive so whoever owned this house must be filthy rich.

"The garden is open to only those who can snag an invite from the family," Hunter whispered in my ear as we rounded a corner. My breath caught when I realized how many people were here. Many were older but I caught a few young faces peering from the crowd. Looking at their dresses and watches I felt extremely underdressed in a white sweater and jeans.

There was a line of tables against the back gate that sat some of the women, while men and other couples seemed to stand at odd areas around the space of the garden and in between the tall bushes of flowers. Waiters walked the area distinguished by their suit and tie along with a tray of drinks and food. This was far out of my league, and I could feel myself shrinking under their gaze.

"How did you get us an invite?" I whispered and took a sip of my coffee hoping to shield my face. People that were staring started to whisper and look us up and down with a distasteful look in their eyes. I hung onto Hunter for dear life. I knew these types of people. When I was playing my role as an escort these people would laugh and joke with me because they assumed I was one of them, but with how I looked now it was only too obvious that I didn't belong here.

"Don't be mad," he said quickly in a low tone. "But I'm going to introduce you to some people."

I froze and snapped my gaze up to Hunter.

"I told you—"

"That you wanted to wait to meet any friends or family until after it has been a year," he said with a sigh. "I know, it's just...*they* insisted."

I didn't want to meet Hunter's friends and family because I didn't know how permanent I wanted this to be. I had been using him during a time of need and just got comfortable with him; I had no intention of actually meeting his family. The fear that I had of him wanting to move forward was not as unfounded as I may have once thought.

"Whose house is this?" I asked, panicked.

"My parents'," he said while clearing his throat and giving me a sheepish look.

This house was his? I swallowed the knot in my throat and tore my eyes away from the mansion that towered over us to our right.

I knew he was rich...*but come on.*

"Hunter," I warned.

"Here they come," he whispered quickly as a couple walked towards us. "Just a warning, my dad is pretty strict Christian."

Jesus, I moaned in my head. *Is this really happening right now?*

"Son," his father said once they reached us.

His father was an aging man with a head full of light brown hair. His green eyes were lined by thick brows, and he had a clean face. It was almost crazy to believe that Hunter had any blood relation to the man in front of me. Instead, he seemed to be an exact male version of his mother. She had the same blond curly hair as he did and bright hazel eyes. She regarded me with a warm smile but the narrowing of her eyes on my outfit did not get past me.

"Father, Mother, I'd like you to meet Jean. My girlfriend," Hunter said with a nervous tone.

"Such a beautiful name," his mother cooed. "My name is Carla, and this is Robert."

"Mr. Williams," Hunter's father corrected.

I hate them already, I thought wryly.

"Mr. Williams, Mrs. Williams, so happy to meet you finally," I lied and put on the sweetest smile that I could muster.

Hunter's arm wrapped around my shoulder and pulled me close.

"Just wanted to stop by while we were in the area," he said with a light tone. "We won't stay for long given that we have a jam-packed schedule today."

I may have been furious with Hunter for bringing me here, but I was happy to see that he at least had some decency to get us out of here soon. By the way his father's eyes roamed over my form with disdain, I couldn't help but think that I wasn't wanted here.

A part of me was surprised that I was not *that* affected by their reaction towards me. If I was a better girlfriend I would be trying to fight for their attention and praise, but I found myself wholly uninterested in it. Instead, it felt much like I was back on the arm of Gary pretending to be his long-term girlfriend and schmoozing the big boss.

I looked up to Hunter with a small, strained smile, playing the part I was supposed to.

This wasn't all fake right? I thought.

He was handsome, caring, great boyfriend, if not husband material...yet something was off. He sent me a dazzling smile as if to ward off those suspicious paranoid thoughts that were nagging at my mind.

At least it wasn't fake to him.

"Well say goodbye to us before you leave," Carla said and pulled her scowling husband away with a wave.

As soon as they were out of sight I turned to Hunter, hiding my face from the crowd of people, and let out a big sigh.

"Jean, listen—"

"What *the fuck* Hunter?" I whispered to him, shooting my eyes around the area hoping no one heard. "You could have at least warned me? How long have you been planning this?"

His hands found my shoulders and he began to knead the tension out of them. If we were at home, I would have smacked his hands away.

"You would have said no," he said in a sad tone. "You know how much they mean to me, and mom has been nonstop asking about you for months."

A couple passed us, greeting Hunter in a cheerful voice. I put on my best fake smile and nodded towards them before looking back towards Hunter.

"So, you bring me to a place where you know I cannot get mad at you, is that it?" I hissed at him.

"Look," he said in a calm voice. "Get mad or not, you could yell at me right now and I wouldn't even care how many people looked. I know why you didn't want to meet them, I do...but it's time. We have been together for almost a year."

"What do you know, Hunter?" I was close to crushing the cup of coffee in my hand or throwing it at him. Throwing it at him would be the more desirable outcome in my current state of mind.

"Family is hard for you since your mom passed and you don't want to throw yourself into another one, essentially erasing her from your life," he said matter-of-factly.

I scoffed at him and shook my head trying to focus on anything other than those stupid words. This had nothing to do with my mother and sure as hell nothing to do with wanting to join his family. Like I would ever want to sit around and flatter these rich people *for free.* At least at the escort job I got paid for that shit.

"Don't get all psychological on me," I hissed at him. "This is about me and you. It has never been about...my mom."

Against my will my voice cracked when mentioning my mom. I cursed internally; I should be over this by now. I've done my grieving.

"There is nothing wrong with us," Hunter said calmly and pulled me into a hug before leading us to a side of the garden where there were less people, and we were hidden by a lemon tree. "This is just the logical next step for us and if nothing is wrong with us then it has to be your feelings about what happened with your mom."

I threw my coffee in a nearby trash can before I could throw it at him. Was he really that blind to not see what is going on? It should be obvious that things are not great between us.

Or maybe it's just seeing Shae that made you doubt things again, a voice in the back of my head whispered. *Maybe you wouldn't have freaked if she didn't come and remind you what you were missing. Maybe it's your fault that you are getting bored.*

It was those thoughts that made me freeze.

It couldn't be Shae, could it? If Hunter had taken me yesterday would I still have been so angry? I swallowed thickly and looked up at him. For the first time in a while, Hunter had a genuine frown on his face.

"I'm sorry," I said finally after a few moments of silence. "You're right there is nothing wrong between us. I am happy we are taking this step, I told you a year and it is almost a year. I shouldn't have gotten angry with you about it."

He gave me a soft smile and leaned down to plant a kiss on my forehead.

"We can leave," he said. "The main point was to meet them

but now that that's over with...how about we get some of that ice cream from the corner store and binge a TV show tonight?"

For real this time, my anger dissipated. How could I say no?

"I would love to," I said with a smile.

I giggled as he pulled me into a tight hug and brought his lips to mine.

Shae

THREE YEARS EARLIER

God this was boring.

I could literally feel my soul draining out of me the longer these imbeciles talked. They both wanted to prove that they had the biggest balls here, but we all knew who was really in charge here and I would be ashamed if I was ever seen acting like this.

"Shae, I can swear to you that I can not only get you double the money this pussy is offering but I guarantee that my transport will be safer, and no one will be able to trace it back to you," Carlos said in a heated voice. His big brown eyes were wide, and I could see the sweat dripping down the side of his neck even in the chilly October air. He was nervous that he was about to lose this deal, as he should be.

I did not give a shit about traceability. I was clean and always had been. Even if they got caught with this shit it wouldn't be my problem, it would be *his* and there was no way that I would be there to clean it up for him.

I exhaled deeply and looked up into the night sky, the stars barely visible with the light pollution in the area. I longed to go to the countryside and see what the *real sky* looked like, though I was sure I would get bored of it in a matter of hours. I turned my attention back to the two in front of me.

As I had requested, they both showed up alone though I had no doubt their bodyguards were around the corner waiting for them. I didn't have anyone waiting for me, but that was also normal. I didn't trust anyone enough to watch my back, not even for all the money in the world. There was always someone else who could find what they wanted and exploit them for it.

At least, if I was by myself I was safe.

The alleyway behind my favorite Chinese place had been a perfect spot for this meeting. It was dark, quiet with only the kitchen noises and cars from a block down. We would not be interrupted. I had foolishly thought that having these two pitted against each other in a small alley would have proved to be somewhat amusing, but alas, they were still boring as hell.

I looked over at Anton. His icy blue eyes were calm, and he gave no indication that he was bothered by the crap Carlos was spewing. In comparison to the man next to him, he was a picture-perfect businessman. I almost thought that he wasn't interested but seeing him still standing here gave me my answer.

"Anton, you know the place," I said and shoved my hands in my jacket pockets. I had placed it over a black hoodie tonight, but I could still feel the cold seeping into me. "Bring your guys next time."

Anton's lips twitched and he nodded to me and then to Carlos. Carlos' mouth dropped open and I could see the veins in his face grow twice as large.

"Shae! Why did you even bring us here if you weren't going to even humor me?" he asked, obviously outraged.

I sent him a smirk.

"I thought it would be funny to see you two fight it out," I said honestly. "Don't worry, your name is still on the next shipment. I heard a Klimt was in there. Newly recovered."

Carlos' body went taunt, and I saw his lips form into a crazed smile.

Man, he would be pissed when he figured out there was no Klimt.

Carlos was the first to move, bidding us both a goodbye. Me with an enthusiastic wave and Anton with a middle finger. I chuckled at his antics.

"Let's go get a drink, my friend," Anton suggested, finally letting a small smile grace his face.

I shook my head and turned toward the other end of the alley.

"I have plans tonight, catch you later," I said with a smile.

"Save that Klimt for me," he called out as I walked away. "*He* won't be needing it soon."

My laugh bounced off the buildings around us. I should have known Anton wouldn't take kindly to being dissed. I sent him a wave a disappeared around the corner.

I checked my phone as I walked down the busy streets of New York, not even paying attention to the people around me. It was late but cars and people were still out, their noises traveling throughout alleys and around corners. One thing I hated—and loved—about New York was just how many people there were. It was never too late for anything, and this was where a business like mine would thrive.

I pulled up the address of the place I was going next onto my phone and smiled, a giggly feeling creeping up inside me. I wasn't normally like this, but I decided that I needed a *different* type of fun in my life. One that was a more rewarding game.

I slipped into a corner coffee shop, warm air blasting my face, chasing away the cold. The warm smell of coffee and baked goods filled the air and clung to the place. I would have never thought a place like this would be open at 1 a.m. but apparently there was a certain type of demand that they couldn't refuse.

My eyes shifted through the area until I found what I was looking for. I had to fight to keep my smile down as I spotted a girl all the way in the corner of the shop, her nose buried in a *really* bulky computer, glasses on her face, dark hair tied up in a bun, and her fingers typing furiously on a keyboard.

Jean.

I hadn't seen her since that drunken night in my house over a month ago and I couldn't get her out of my head. It hadn't taken long to track her down. Sweet Caroline had given me her full name and social media accounts and since then it had been easy to figure out her habits.

Jean Taylor. 24. Habitually unemployed. Dead broke. Currently escorting every other week.

She had a thing for coffee and apparently visited this place almost every night.

I walked up to the counter and ordered a black coffee before watching her from the bar. I wouldn't approach, yet. I just wanted to watch as she fussed over whatever it was she was working on.

She was so focused that she didn't even feel me staring and just continued to stare daggers at her computer. When her eyebrows smushed together I found myself smiling. Before she gave herself a headache I walked over to her table and pulled up a chair loudly. She jumped and stared at me with a shocked expression as I sat down.

"Shae?" Her voice was hoarse as if just getting over a cold.

"Fancy seeing you here, Jean," I said in a low voice as I took a sip of my coffee. It was far too bitter and tasted like the boy at the counter had burned it.

Her cheeks flushed an adorable looking red as she stuttered.

"Do you come here often?" she asked while looking up at me through her lashes.

"That's a lame pick-up line," I said. "You should try harder than that if you want an invitation back to my apartment."

For the first time, I saw a flash of anger cross her face and her lips formed a small pout.

"I don't want to go back to your apartment," she said with a huff. "I was just trying to make conversation."

"Sure, you were," I teased. "What are you doing out here so late?"

She sighed, the anger seeming to disappear with her breath, and slouched back in her chair. She pushed up her glasses rubbing the bridge of her nose.

"I have been lagging on my courses and am trying to rush to finish them," she explained. "I have been here almost every night this week, which is why I am surprised to only see you here now."

Courses while being broke as fuck, does she really think that is going to change anything?

"I was in the area and needed a place to put my feet up," I lied. "What are you studying? I didn't know you were still in school."

She sat straight, rolling her neck as she did so. I couldn't help but watch as she did. I remembered how it felt under my hand as she screamed.

"I graduated a few years back," she said and shifted her glasses back onto her face, looking me straight in the eyes. There was no blush this time. *Interesting.* "For a stupid major and I was thinking while I had a chance I might as well get certificates to beef up my resume."

I nodded before smirking at her.

"I didn't know escorts needed a resume," I joked barely keeping the chuckle out of my voice.

Again, I saw the agitation line her face.

"Caroline told me about you, you know?" Her tone was snarky. "She told me how you like to push people's buttons and think you are above everyone else."

I quirked my brow at her. "Oh yeah?"

"Yeah! And how you think you're some big art dealer but really you are a low-level *thug* that schmoozes people for money and uses it to get girls to bend over for you." Her voice was loud enough to get the three people in there to turn towards us. She seemed to shrink under the attention, but it only stroked my ego.

I leaned forward and slammed her computer shut. She jumped and opened her mouth to berate me, but I dove forward and gripped her cheeks, stopping her from speaking.

"Are you mad I didn't ask for your number after I fucked you in my bathroom?" I asked in a sweet voice.

When she tried to speak again it came out jumbled. Her hands clawed at my arm, but I kept my grip firm on her face.

"Or is it that Caroline told you about my sex life and you finally realized that you are nothing more than a number on my list?" I leaned my head forward, almost as if to kiss her. Her eyes widened but this time she didn't push me away, instead pulled me closer. "Being jealous is a good look on you, love."

I leaned back and pushed her away. She crossed her arms over her chest and sent me a glare. I looked her up and down realizing how little she was wearing. A t-shirt and jeans in the middle of October.

"You don't need to be a dick," she hissed and brought the once frozen—now melted—drink to her lips.

"What certificate are you working on?" I asked her as I shrugged off my coat and folded it into my lap.

She gave me a look before answering, "Interior design."

My research never yielded an interest in interior design.

"You don't look like someone who is into interior design," I noted.

"I watched house renovation shows with my mom when I was younger," she said with a smile. "I thought that it may be fun so I looked up how to become one and found out not only do they make a lot of money but there are also courses you can take instead of getting a master's or bachelor's degree."

"If it's money you should just keep escorting," I said. "What, you make like a few thousand every night?"

Caroline had said two thousand on a good night.

She nodded but grimaced.

"It's not my favorite job," she said in a small voice. "Most of the men are annoying. Like yeah I get to go to nice places, get good money and tips...but it's just not my thing, y'know? They get grabby sometimes and there are some that are just so god damn *disgusting.*"

I had never before snorted in a conversation, but her response pulled a laugh out of me that I wasn't expecting.

"Yeah, men are like that," I said with a sigh and paused for a moment while looking at her. "I may have an idea for your money issues."

She raised an eyebrow at me and a frown graced her beautifully plump lips.

"Nothing illegal," she warned. I shook my head.

"It's totally legal," I said in a smug tone. "And I really wouldn't call it a job..."

She leaned forward as I trailed off.

"Well?"

"I'm in need of some entertainment," I said finally. Her face fell for a moment before I saw the wheels turning in her head, then she met me back with a fierce look.

"You don't have to pay me for sex," she whispered. "That's not what I do."

I rolled my eyes.

"Let me rephrase," I said. "I am in need of someone to *spoil*."

She looked around the coffee shop as if we were having an illicit conversation. It made my heart speed up because I knew at this moment she wouldn't say no to me, and I had been dreaming about this interaction for a month straight.

"A sugar baby?" she asked.

"Or a girlfriend," I proposed. "Whatever you want to call it."

She took another sip of that disgusting drink while thinking it over.

"How would it work?" she asked.

Gotcha. I thought to myself. *Too easy.*

"Simple," I said. "We see each other multiple times a week, have dinner, have sex and I supply you with whatever you need. Want me to pay for that course? I'll do it. Want a new car? You got it. *Anything.*"

I could tell she wasn't breathing by how stiff her posture was.

Then like a switch a sly smile spread across her face, and she leaned back in her chair.

"That's a *big commitment*," she mused. "I'm not sure I'm ready for that."

A smirk spread across my own face as I stood up. Her panicked expression was all too sweet.

"No commitment, we end it when we want to," I said. "Hell, we can even fuck other people if you want, but I have a feeling we won't need that." I sent her a wink and tossed my jacket to her. "Let me know and when you are ready, my number is in the jacket pocket."

I turned to walk away but her voice caught me.

"A car," she said in a sure voice. "Get me one by this weekend and have it delivered to my door."

I turned to her, a feeling of excitement running through me. When I looked back at her she was leaning forward her elbows on the table and her head in her hands with a sickly sweet smile aimed towards me.

"Get me a car," she repeated. "So, I know you won't go back on your words and I'll consider your offer."

Consider? Ha!

She was going to be much more interesting than I first thought.

"You got it, love," I said. "Be on the lookout for it."

I walked away ignoring her as she called after me.

"Don't you want my address?!" was the last thing I heard before I left the cafe and walked into the cold morning air.

Jean

After the run-in with his parents, Hunter had taken steps to become even sweeter and more overbearing than he was before. I tried to revel in the attention, in the love. But after some time, it got suffocating and I could no longer stand it. My smiles were forced and at times it felt like this was a full-time escort job.

I laughed when I was supposed to.

Smiled when I was supposed to.

Acted like nothing was wrong.

Yet every day I would wake up to breakfast and then regardless of the time he would drive me to work, two days of the week he would even meet me at my office for lunch and it was enough to make me suspicious of his motives. The office ladies loved it and gossiped like crazy.

I had heard their whispers, and although they didn't sting... they were not pleasant.

She pregnant, they would say loudly behind their hands.

He obviously has money, she's a gold digger, they would whisper behind the dividers that separated our desks.

They would giggle loudly when they saw us leave together almost like they wanted me to hear what they were saying.

I wasn't close to them, nor did I ever tell them about my relationship so of course they would speculate. I tried to keep myself distanced from them. After all, a job was a job, and I wouldn't get close to someone like *Gary* so why would I even bother with these girls?

"God," Amber said with a sigh as she watched Hunter wave to me from the entrance of our building. We had just come back from a quick lunch at a cafe down the street and he made a show of kissing me deeply in front of my coworkers before leaving. "If you don't marry that man I will."

I rolled my eyes at her. She was the one I was most friendly with, but I didn't kid myself by thinking that we were even acquaintances. At this point we were just two people who shared the same hell of working at this soul-sucking company.

"It's a little early to be thinking about that," I explained as I swiped my badge on the card reader to the elevator. "We've only been together for a year next month."

Amber gave me a look that told me I was crazy.

"Aren't you and I like the same age?" she asked with a huff. "Your internal clock is counting down. A year is plenty of time for you to figure out if the relationship would work."

"Please don't talk to me about my biological clock," I said with a groan.

My phone vibrated in my pocket, and I motioned for Amber to get on the elevator without me. She gave me a questioning look as the elevator doors closed but I continued to just wave her off.

"Already?" I asked Caroline as soon as it was safe.

"Are you really complaining about money?" she said over the phone, her southern drawl more pronounced than ever. It tended to come out when she was angry. "If so I'll get another girl to do it."

I covered my face with my hand and let out a sigh. Last week had come and gone and it had been exhausting trying to regulate my emotions around Hunter, especially since he was being so extra lately. Every time I met his eyes I felt like guilt would explode from inside me and I either wanted to throw everything away and leave for good or fall to my knees and beg him to forgive me.

Getting money for unpaid medical bills was one thing but doing it as an escort *and* running into my ex-girlfriend in the bathroom was something else entirely. There were many times where I would wake up in the middle of the night from a dream about her once again, exploring my body and hoping that Hunter could make me forget about it...but more often than not he left me unsatisfied and wishing for more.

"No," I said with a heavy sigh. "I need it. When is it?"

"Tomorrow night," she said with a tone I couldn't make out. "They *really* want it to be you so please tell me you have time. I was kidding about going to get another girl."

"How much?" I asked and loaded into the elevator alone. It had a sweaty smell that caused me to almost gag.

"Three grand," she said.

I mused over the idea. It was good pay, better than even Gary could manage. I was still around sixty thousand dollars in debt but at least what I made this month would be enough to tide over the insane interest payment. When I checked my balance as of last week it seemed like it had almost doubled in size after just a few months of not paying.

I had to fork over a lot of money for repairs on the apartment and it left nothing for the payments. And of course, I couldn't let Hunter know just how much I needed money, so I was left to stew in my debt-filled anxiety alone.

"Where?" I asked looking at the bright fluorescents that lit the slowly moving elevator. I was on the twelfth floor. I had little time for this conversation and no way in hell was I letting those gossiping ladies get one up on me.

"I'll give you a ride," she said. "I will provide the outfit if you bring me back the mini I lent you."

"I'll be over after work tomorrow," I said and hung up just as the doors opened.

The rest of the day went by in the blink of an eye. I worked on a few new marketing projects, onboarded a client, and overall just kept my head down and focused on work. It was not fun work, but it was busy. It paid the bills and I was good at it, that's all that mattered.

This was one of the only full-time jobs that I could get with my marketing degree and almost zero experience. I had once thought that I could be an interior designer; my mom had absolutely loved the thought…but it never worked out.

Between everything that happened with Shae, and my mother being admitted…I couldn't bring myself to put myself out there for a job I had no idea if I would be good at or not. So I just stuffed the cheap certificate in my closet and forgot about it.

It was better that way. Not everything could be as intoxicating and dangerous as working with Shae was. I remember the times she would bring me to work with her, the thrill it would send up my spine and the adrenaline that would pump through my veins. It was as exciting as it was exhausting.

At least this work was boring and predictable. This was real life and whatever I had been doing before this was behind me now.

When my phone rang the next time, it was Hunter telling me he was already waiting for me downstairs. He was earlier than usual, but I would take whatever excuse I got to finally make my escape. My mind already felt numb from the day's dull work and I was ready for a break, even if it meant dealing with Hunter's extreme emotions as of late.

With a wave to Amber and a few others I made my way to the parking garage only to see Hunter waiting for me outside the car with a bouquet of lilac-colored roses. I gave him a small forced smile.

Weren't the last ones still dying on our kitchen counter?

"What's with all the pampering lately, huh?" I asked playfully and stretched to give him a kiss on the lips.

"You deserve it," he said with an air of confidence, his hazel eyes bright and playful. At least his job seemed to be more enjoyable than mine. "And I am taking you out tonight."

"It's a Thursday," I said with a nervous laugh and took the fragrant flowers into my arms. Hunter may have come from money but never had he showered me with gifts like this before and with the way he was pushing our relationship... I could only guess what the next steps were.

"Out to eat," he said with a smile. "We can go out to the bars tomorrow if you are feeling up to it."

I stilled when I remembered where I had to be tomorrow.

"Actually Caroline already reserved my Friday for me," I said trying not to fidget. "She is going through a breakup right now and needs some moral support."

Hunter's lips turned downward but he nodded nonetheless.

"Saturday then," he said and moved to open the car door for me. "Until tomorrow, you are all mine." He sent me a wink as I lowered myself into the seat before shutting the car door and running to the other side.

"So where are we going?" I asked as he pulled out of my company's parking garage.

"Someplace small," he replied with a grin.

HUNTER and I had two very different ideas of the word small.

I thought he was going to bring me to a quaint little restaurant where we could chat and relax, but instead he brought me straight to a rooftop bar in the middle of Manhattan. There was music going, people were chatting loudly, and I was definitely not in dress code. My work was casual so I had chosen a cardigan and high-waisted jeans but everyone else was wearing short dresses and button-downs even in this chilly weather.

So much for a nice quiet chat, I thought bitterly.

"Why didn't you warn me," I hissed at Hunter.

He didn't look at all fazed and just continued to push us forward with a smile. The hostess received us with a glowing smile and even checked Hunter out as if I was not holding onto his arm. He seemed to swell under the attention and...it didn't even bother me. He was just that type of person, loved to be in the limelight and was literally like a shining star whenever he spoke. He gave her his name and right away we were taken to a not-so-secluded area right near the edge of the rooftop.

It was breathtaking, don't get me wrong. With lights strung all over us, plants elegantly placed between each table, it was a place I may have loved to go...if I was ready. Now that I was here, I found myself woefully unprepared with my stomach in knots. Not only was there way more people and noise than I expected, but our seat put us right near the edge of the rooftop and there was no getting past the deadly drop to the bustling city streets below.

While there may have been a large glass wall that towered over us and kept us in place, my nerves did not notice a difference. It was the same as if I was standing right on the edge looking down for myself.

I barely noticed Hunter ordering and didn't even look at him until the waitress put down our wine on the table, I was too busy trying—and failing—to not look down at the street below. I jumped at the movement and Hunter gave me a pinched expression.

"Heights," I explained sheepishly and took a generous gulp of the white wine. "Been scared since I was a child."

He nodded and relaxed in his chair.

"I was scared of the ocean," he said. "Still am sometimes."

I took a sip of the wine with a shaky hand and forced a smile to my face. *He was trying at least,* I thought.

"What's so scary about the ocean?" I asked in a teasing tone. He raised a blond eyebrow at me.

"What's so scary about heights?" he said back.

I rolled my eyes.

"Certain death," I shot back.

"Same with the ocean," he said playfully. "Sharks, drowning, you name it."

"But not certain," I said leaning forward. "If you learn to swim you will survive, and besides sharks aren't the issue here, that's their home. Shark attacks are uncommon."

"People fly all the time, hell our apartment is on the sixth floor. Heights is not so certain either," he said with a smile.

I took a sip of my wine feeling much better than before. This was what I liked about Hunter, he was genuinely a nice person and knew what I needed to distract me.

"If you get thrown off a building you will die; if you get thrown into water you can live," I said and raised my eyebrow, daring him to fight me.

"I guess you win," he said with a sigh. "How was work today? You barely texted me."

I let out a sigh.

"I think it's time to find something new," I said seriously. "I'm tired of picking up the slack for everyone. And it's just *so boring.*"

Hunter looked out into the city around us. He tapped his finger on his wine glass.

"You could quit," he suggested. "I think I may know a place that's hiring."

A glimmer of hope rose in my chest.

"Really?" I asked. "Where? I'd do anything to get out of this boring ass work."

He took a sip of his wine still not looking at me.

"My father's place..."

Only then did his eyes slide across to mine. I sat back with an uneasy feeling in my stomach.

"*Mr. Williams* doesn't like me," I said not able to keep the venom out of my tone. Hunter let out a sigh and ran a hand through his curly locks, obviously uncomfortable.

"He's like that with everyone," he said. "I am serious though,

I could ask him and he would give a recommendation to the marketing head in minutes."

I sipped my wine pretending to be thoughtful but inside my mind was a flurry of panic.

He's doing this to help me right?

I feel like this is too much of a step, getting too close to him and his family.

Oh god, he doesn't know about the escorting does he?

I looked over him carefully, he was watching me just as closely as I was watching him.

"I don't know..."

"It's okay," he said too quickly. "It's just an option to fall back on, in case you *really* hate your job."

I nodded.

"It's also a close-knit company," I said remembering when he told me literally everyone in his family had worked there at one time or another. Cousins, aunts, uncles, everyone with an ounce of Williams blood was welcome. It was something like a rite of passage. "Wouldn't want to disrupt that."

He leaned over and grasped my hand in his. I hadn't realized how cold my hands were until his warm ones engulfed mine.

"You are family, Jean," he said sincerely.

My breath caught.

The waitress chose that moment to save me from my impending doom by sliding over with our plates. A steak for Hunter and a Caesar salad for me. With a dry mouth I slowly ate my food, not feeling very hungry anymore.

There was something about this whole thing that didn't feel right to me. The air was too expectant, his words were too odd for someone like him. I would like to pride myself on thinking that I know Hunter well. We had been together for almost a year and if I didn't know him by now...

We ate silently. It was awkward and tense. I knew he expected me to respond to him but, I wasn't good at this. As an escort I was prepared to act but here, in real life with *real* feelings involved, I had no way to navigate this type of relationship with Hunter.

He obviously wanted more, always had. It was me who had been reluctant to get into this relationship...but it would be a cheap shot if I didn't give it my all.

"Thank you," I said after I finished my salad. "For the dinner, for the gifts, for your words." I reached across the table and threaded my fingers through his. "It means a lot to me and I will think about your offer."

His face lit up instantly. He lifted my hand and brought it to his lips.

"I really meant it Jean, I want you to be happy," he said with a light smile. "I can do that. Whether it be the job, or taking you out, or even a place if we want to..."

He trailed and I shifted uncomfortably under his gaze.

"I appreciate it Hunter," I said, smiling at him. "You have been here from the beginning and I know I couldn't have done this past year without you."

"I couldn't have done it without you, really," he said.

This was a lot, I thought but swallowed my pride anyways.

"This was nice Hunter," I said after a moment. "Thanks for taking us."

"I think we should treat ourselves to dessert," he said with an excited tone. "They have a tiramisu to die for."

"Between the breakfast, lunch, and now dinner... I'm stuffed," I said with a laugh and dramatically patted my stomach.

His face dropped slightly.

"I think you would *really* like it," he said in a tone that sounded like I should know what he was hinting at, but I had no idea.

"I'm sure I would," I said, slightly uncomfortable again. "But my wonderful boyfriend has been feeding me non-stop today, I'm not sure how I would fit it."

I let out a light laugh to soften the mood but his eyes darted over to the waitstaff that was currently standing by the bar, his eyes on our table. He stood up straight when he met Hunter's gaze, nodded, then left to go back inside where the kitchens were located.

Oh shit, I thought. *This isn't what I think it is, is it?*

"Let's go Hunter," I said in a low voice, trying to play it cool. "I want to treat you as well tonight."

I lifted his hand and placed a small kiss on his wrist before biting it softly. I watched as he swallowed and a panic crossed his face.

"Babe," he whined softly.

I licked the spot I bit and gave him a hooded look. I prayed to god he would cave, though I knew it wouldn't take long. Hunter was just as horny as the next guy.

"Let's get out of here then," he said quickly, his voice rough. "I'll pay for the dinner, go wait for me in the car."

I stood with him, relieved, and took his keys from him with a grateful smile. He waved me off with a tense look as I walked to the car.

When I was out of sight I let out a deep sigh, feeling the tension in my shoulders leave with it. I wanted to chalk everything up to my anxiety but if it wasn't... I would have sworn he was about to propose. It would only make sense.

The treatment.

The gifts.

Meeting the parents.

I entered the elevator and checked my phone, trying to distract my mind from everything. There was a glaring notification on my screen that made everything with Hunter feel minuscule.

A missed call from my beloved father. My eyes stung when I thought of him, and not because I missed him. If anything I hated him more than life itself and he only called for one reason.

He was the lucky one in this relationship. He didn't have to deal with mom's sickness or the bills afterwards. He had left right when mom was taking a turn for the worse with barely a goodbye.

Mom took it well and laughed and joked the whole time, but I was fuming. During the time he left I had pretended, for her, that I was okay with everything but swallowing everything had only seemed to deepen the hate.

He had a new family with kids and everything. I was twice their age and their mother was barely older than I was. He didn't even want me to meet them; he refused when I had asked. Maybe he knew I asked out of spite and that was why he refused, but that didn't stop me from finding them.

They had a cute little house in the suburbs—one that my mother and him could never afford—and they were the picture-perfect family. I watched them for days as they went on about their life. He would take the younger boys to school while his new wife stayed home with a swollen belly.

It was pitiful and disgusting.

Nonetheless, he was still my father so I lifted the phone to my ear and listened to his voicemail.

"Um Jean, wanted to let you know that the insurance contacted me again about the past due payment. I see you made a payment on the account not too long after they called but wanted to let you know that they were um...more forceful this time and let me know if you didn't pay *all* the late fees, that they would need to look into repossession and uh...a hold on your card." There was a pause on the other line. Maybe a whisper?

Probably his kids. I'm sure if they were in this situation he wouldn't hesitate to fork over the money.

"I thought you should know," he finished and hung up the phone.

I was tempted to throw my phone at the ground and stomp on it until it shattered into a million pieces, but that would just be another expense for me to pay. With heavy breathing and a pain in my chest I stormed out of the elevator as soon as the doors opened.

The late fees alone were like ten thousand dollars after not paying for so long and even then, they kept accumulating because

I was never able to pay off the minimum amount they required. *How the fuck did they think I was going to repay that? And they had my information on file, why would they call my dad?* He has not paid a single bill since she died.

I braced myself on the side of Hunter's car, the pain in my chest intensifying. The cardigan became itchy and the underground parking felt like it was closing in on me. This was impossible. Even if I took all the escorting jobs in the world I wouldn't be able to pay it back as fast as they needed me to.

"Jean?" Hunter's concerned voice rang out from behind me. His large hand cupped my shoulder and turned me around to face him. His eyebrows pushed together and his hand came up to my cheeks. "Why are you crying?"

I wiped away my tears quickly and let out a pitiful laugh.

"Dad called," I said in a bitter tone. "Doesn't want to pay the hospital fees."

Hunter knew I was in debt but he didn't know how bad it was. I would never let him know the massive debt I was in. It was embarrassing and my responsibility alone to pay it back. On top of that, I really didn't want to owe anyone ever again... I was my own adult now and I could do this. I *had* to do this. He had already done enough already, seeing me through the thick of my grief after my mom passed away.

It was the reason we became so close in the first place.

"That bastard," he said and pulled me closer to him. "Do you need...?"

I shook my head then buried it into his chest inhaling his scent. I felt my body relax slowly as he rubbed soothing circles in my back. This was the Hunter I originally thought would be a good person to be with. I wouldn't say that I ever truly loved him, but I was sure that would be able to grow into it. I think I still can.

"I know it's hard but don't think too much about him," he said and placed a kiss on the top of my head. "Let's go home and we can cuddle on the couch while we watch something on HGTV."

I let out a laugh.

"You hate HGTV," I said with a laugh.

"But you *love* those stupid shows no matter how fake and cringe they are and if that's what will make my baby feel better then we do it," he said and moved to open the door.

I leaned up and gave him a kiss, the earlier proposal officially forgotten.

Shae

I didn't mean for her to stay the night.

At least the first time I didn't. But now we were on night thirty-something and I couldn't bring myself to force her to leave. As I watched her bring more and more stuff in I merely smiled and let her move in what she wanted. I never really stood and thought what it meant to have her in here. What it meant to have her slowly invade my space and every other part of my being.

Or at least I didn't until this morning.

"I think I will break my lease if you are cool with me staying here," she said with a casual tone but I could see the look in her eyes and how she fidgeted in her seat.

She was nervous, I thought, amused at her actions. Where was the little tiger that demanded I got her a car before we fucked again?

In part, I liked that I made her nervous, but another part of me was bored. That was such an expected reaction from girls nowadays. You get along, sleep over a few times, and suddenly they are ready to move in. My mind went straight to a breakup, but a part of my chest tugged when I realized that would mean I would never see her again.

I liked her. Liked the feel of her skin against mine. Liked her warmth.

"As long as you don't mind when I bring chicks over," I said with a smirk.

A beautifully angry flush exploded in her cheeks and her smile changed into a defined pout. This was my favorite reaction. Even now it made a heat awaken in my belly.

"I've been here for over almost two months and haven't seen you bring in a girl or even text another one," she said with her own smirk and proud look on her face.

"Like I could let my side pieces see each other," I joked. "Are you trying to get me killed?"

She quirked an eyebrow at me before throwing back her head and letting out a laugh that warmed the empty space immediately. I had meticulously filled my space with the best most expensive furniture and made sure it was constantly clean. Some people called it sterile and cold...but I had never thought of it that way. I thought of it as just another way to show off my possessions.

That was until Jean started coming in and throwing her shit everywhere. Clothes that were not mine hung in the closet. Stupid dollar knickknacks littered the kitchen, and I always caught her bringing home another. The hallways that were once desolate were now lit up with laughter and my bed never felt cold anymore.

After she came into my life, I realized I quite liked the warmth.

"Tell her thanks for keeping the bed warm," she said and leaned across the table to give me a kiss on the lips. "I'll tell mine the same thing."

Faster than I even realized, my hand wrapped around her neck and I pulled her close to me, forcing her lips back to mine as I ravished them. Biting at her, sucking the swollen flesh into my mouth. She was whimpering by the time I pulled away. She glared at me with light tears in her eyes and her swollen lips formed into another pout.

"Get over to the window," I demanded.

She cocked her head to the side like a damn dog and gave me a doe-eyed expression. I sighed and let go of her throat only to take her hand and drag her to the place she hated the most.

"Shae you know I don't like to get too close—" I cut her off by pushing her against the glass. Her eyes screwed shut so hard I was sure she would be seeing stars when they opened. I pushed her head slightly harder into the glass. She let out an uncomfortable cry and her legs were already shaking.

"If you didn't like it you shouldn't have been a brat," I hissed.

"You started it!" she cried and tried to grab a hold of my arm but failed miserably with her eyes still screwed shut.

"Take it back," I growled. I knew that it bothered me, that much was easy to understand but the more I thought about it the angrier I got... How dare she make me feel these things? How dare she make me change into something I didn't recognize?

"You have to take it back too," she said in a weak voice. "Shae let me up, I'm going to fall."

I rolled my eyes and quickly dipped my hands into the front of her pants without waiting. Her gasp pushed me forward and my fingers easily slid through her folds.

"You like to be scared," I noted and pulled out my hand. My fingers were glistening in the morning sun. I put my hand in front of her face. "Look."

Slowly she opened her eyes to look at my glimmering fingers. I brought them to her lips and let out a groan as her tongue dutifully lapped up every drop.

"I like to be controlled," she corrected, her eyes shifting back towards mine. "By you."

The burst of warmth from my chest was not the type of arousal but I ignored it.

~

ON NIGHT eighty-seven was when I knew for the second time that I had fucked up.

Jean was more gorgeous the more that I got to know her. By this time I found her utterly irresistible and even when she wasn't with me, I would constantly be checking on her through her phone messages or even showing up to her outings.

I would remain hidden and out of sight, but I just felt such a pull to her that whenever I was away I had no choice but to follow her.

She was escorting that night. I followed her to a special gala that was put on by a colleague of mine, but she didn't know that... and neither did her date. She was working the crowd as usual, and looking absolutely beautiful in that slim-fitting dress. They stood near the wall chatting to some people I didn't recognize. I made sure to sit in the opposite corner so I could keep a good eye on her.

As if she could feel the eyes on her, her eyes snapped to mine. Her face turned that beautiful red that I loved, but she did not dare move from her post, instead she fanned her face and continued to walk around on his arm.

When I left and went home, she followed not long after me and when she walked in the door she was ready to fight.

"You need to stay away from my job," she hissed and slammed the door behind her.

I rolled my eyes and poured myself a drink from the bar.

"You don't need that job," I reminded. "I thought we agreed you would quit."

She huffed and stormed across the room to grab the drink out of my hands, then downed it in one gulp.

"*You* said I don't need the job. *I* didn't agree to that," she said her voice raising an octave. "It's the only thing I have left!"

I raised a brow at her.

"What do you mean the *only thing* you have left?" I gestured to the penthouse around us. "You literally have everything you could ever want."

She brought down the cup on the counter with a loud smack.

"I mean that it's the only thing that's *my* thing," she said. "Everything else is yours. The car, the house, the clothes, the money...well most. It's just the only thing I can do myself."

"Are you saying you don't like everything I have given you?" I growled.

She glared at me.

"That's not what I mean and you know it."

"That's what it sounds like," I pointed out.

"It's just if I lose my job, I feel like I'm not my own person anymore," she said, her eyes begging me.

I let a small smile come to my face and stroked the side of her cheek.

"Quit by tomorrow or I will quit for you," I threatened.

I left her in a state of shocked silence.

ON NIGHT ninety-three was when I knew that I was fucked.

It was late into the night, almost early in the morning when I turned over and whispered lazily in her ear. It was normal for us to spend the night ravishing each other and sleep just as the morning was upon us.

The silence of the world and the warmth of her body against mine created this perfect little world for us to get lost in. The outside didn't matter. The insecurities and distrust of the world seemed to melt away the further our bodies melded together.

It was my own lost mind that caused me to slip up.

For a long time I chalked it up to the tiredness of that night, but a part of me always knew that I had been wide awake *and* conscious of my choice of words. It was just another way to shake off my embarrassment, I was self-aware enough to know that now.

Jean had been open about her affections and so when she whispered, "I love you..."

...I thought nothing of it. If anything, I was used to the hints that were being dropped and even have heard those same words whispered to me many times before.

A part of me loved it.

I was not a child who grew up in a house full of love or warmth. I had to fend for myself for the most time in empty houses and had yearned for someone to love me like Jean would... but I never thought that I was even capable of loving someone back. Nor did I really want to.

Call it selfish but I wanted to feel the love, not give it. I wanted to hoard all of the warmth it caused inside me, and feared that letting my own love slip out of me would leave me with nothing else. I didn't want to be left with that cold feeling ever again and therefore giving it scared the shit out of me. Even just the thought of it caused my stomach to twist and my hands to shake.

But when I smiled into her and kissed her cheek, the warmth got to me. I had been too hungry, too selfish with my love and it finally found a way out of me. My mouth opened by itself.

"I love you too," I whispered against her.

We both froze. She opened her mouth to speak but I stopped her before she could utter a word. Stopped her before she ruined it. Stopped her before she had a chance to steal the warmth inside me.

"Don't."

Jean

I had cried all night, even after Hunter had gone to sleep. For some reason the tears just wouldn't stop coming until it was already two in the morning. At that point they had begun to dry and a different type of emotion bubbled up inside of me.

Instead, I didn't take this as an insult or as something that should freeze me in my path. This was a sign that I needed to work harder. I had the means and the capability to make this money, now I just needed to put in the work.

"Don't stay out too late tonight," Hunter teased as he dropped me off at work the next morning. "I have a surprise planned for us tomorrow morning that requires you to be clear-headed and fully awake."

I raised my eyebrow at him.

"Do tell," I teased back and leaned in for a small kiss.

"Do you not know the meaning of a surprise?" he asked with a chuckle and deepened our kiss.

I tried to pull away but he wrapped his fingers in my hair and pulled me closer. It was possessive and demanding and just what I needed from him. I let out a small moan and melted into him. He pulled away just as I felt a heat build inside me. "Be good and I'll see you later tonight."

I swallowed thickly and nodded before collecting my bag and leaving the car. I waved him off as he went, wishing that he could have stayed just a moment longer. I wouldn't deny a quickie in the car.

"God that was hot," Amber commented from behind me.

I jumped at the sound of her voice and gave her a glare.

"Peeping Tom much?" I teased. She only rolled her eyes at me and twirled a strand of her hair.

"You were making out in front of a corporate building," she said. "It's fair game, luckily the higher-ups didn't see you."

I shook my head and pulled out my phone.

"Go on ahead of me," I said. "Have to make a call."

She looked me up and down but said nothing as she walked back into the building. I lifted my phone to my ear just in time to hear Caroline's shriek.

"You better not fucking cancel," she hissed through the phone. I winced at the volume.

"I *am not* canceling," I said in a calming voice. "I am actually calling to ask for more."

"More what?" she said hesitantly.

"Hours, dumbass," I hissed at her. "It could be the client tonight or another one, I don't care. Hell even throw Gary in there. Just anything."

There was a pause on the other line.

"Are you...okay, girl?" she asked slowly. "Did Hunter kick you out or something?"

"Mom's medical bills," I explained. She let out a hiss.

"Blood suckers."

"Draining every last drop," I said and began walking into the building.

"I'll see what I can do," she said. "What time will you be over?"

"Five-ish," I replied as I scanned my badge to the elevator.

"Sounds good," she said. "I'll text you if I have any updates."

"Thanks, see ya."

I shifted my stance and held my head a little higher as I walked into the elevator.

Today would be a good day, I vowed. *It would be the first step into fixing the shit hole I am in and after I have done what I can... I will leave this behind forever.*

~

So as it would turn out, today would not be a good day.

The clients I onboarded the day before got cold feet and decided to fight us on their plan, stating that I had misled them about the costs of our services. Which was obviously not true; I had a feeling they were price hunting and wanted to see how low we could go but this wasn't a fucking bargain hut. They would get what they would get, or at least that's what I tried to say in a polite corporate tone. My boss digressed.

I spilled coffee on my shirt, twice, all before lunch. And on top of that I had to stay late so when it was time to get to Caroline's I was running into her studio panting and sweating like crazy...at 6 o'clock.

"Get your ass in the back," she hissed as she opened the shop's door for me. "The client is expecting you to be there in ten minutes."

I pushed my way past her and ran to the changing room that housed a vanity, an entire closet, and more makeup than I could ever afford in my life. There was enough room in here for multiple girls to get ready at once but there was rarely a need for that many at a time. Clients tended to have favorites so tonight I would be in here alone.

The entire shop was a quaint studio that she had bought to help run her business. Rumor was that it used to be a small deli and that was why there were sometimes weird dark stains on the concrete floors and back walls... I didn't think too hard about what else it could be. All that mattered was that it was discreet and no one from the outside would even care to look at it or know what was really going on behind the storefront.

I changed into the skintight dark green dress that she laid out for me. It was silky and soft to the touch. It looked like she was going big tonight—the material alone felt more than this job was worth. I twisted my hair into a somewhat acceptable style before scrambling for makeup. Caroline showed up in the mirror behind me with a scowl on her face.

"I forgot your dress," I muttered brushing on some powder. She waved me off.

"I hope they don't get angry," she muttered.

"Where is it?" I asked as I applied a nude lipstick. The setting powder had all but absorbed my sweat and the hairstyle looked just a bit out of place, but I was hoping that gave a sultry vibe rather than a I-was-late vibe. *This would work*, I thought to myself as I brushed off the excess powder. All clients were the same, just needed a woman to bat their eyelashes at them and laugh at their jokes.

"MOMA," she replied in a bored tone.

"Are you kidding me?" I asked my voice raising an octave. "That's too far to make it!"

"I know," she said with an eye roll. "That's why we need to rush."

"We will still be late," I said and transferred my phone and wallet from my bag to another one that matched my dress a bit more.

"Grab your shoes and let's go," she said with a growl and left me alone in the room to scramble to find matching shoes in my size.

THIRTY MINUTES LATER, after running almost two red lights and sweeping in and out of traffic, I finally made it to the art museum. Caroline had pushed me out of the car with only short clipped sentences and then was off to break more traffic rules, almost hitting an old lady as she sped away.

When I finally got to catch my breath I looked around trying to spot my client but there was nothing out of the ordinary. Normally we would have done an introduction and some background before embarking on this journey but here I was stranded with nothing.

They will see you and approach, as they have requested, Caroline had said to me before we arrived.

No one here looked as though they were looking for their date. Most seemed to already have a date and there was an excited chattering amongst the small crowds as they came and left the museum. All of them were dressed similarly to myself so I assumed there must have been an event going on.

Of course there was, my thoughts said in a venomous tone. *Why else would they need you?*

"Beautiful," a sultry voice came from behind me.

I knew that voice... *Of course* I knew that voice. It was the same one that had been in haunting my dreams leaving me horny and filled with guilt. The same one that wouldn't leave no matter how hard I wished for it to. And now it was here to haunt me once again.

"Do you really have to follow me everywhere?" I asked as I turned around to glare at Shae.

God damnit.

She looked fucking amazing in that suit. Her dark eyes were alight with mischief and she had a smirk already plastered on her face. Her hair was fully slicked back except for the one stray hair that hung on the right side of her face. She wore an all-black suit with a dark green satin button-up underneath...and of course the first like four buttons had to be undone. My mouth dried when I saw that she was wearing a gold body chain that went up the middle of her chest and wrapped around her throat.

She let out a chuckle.

"Like what you see?" she asked and stepped closer dipping her head so she could whisper in my ear. "Maybe if you're good tonight I can show you more."

My breath caught in my throat and my skin heated up unbearably. Against what my body wanted, I stepped away and glared at her.

"Like I'd ever want to see that again," I said in a cool voice. "I have enough PTSD from our last interaction to last me a lifetime."

She let out a scoff and threw her arm around my shoulder. A gesture too casual too fast that made my mind spiral back to what it was like to be with her again.

"Let's go, love."

I tried to stop her from pushing me forward but in these tiny heels it was barely a deterrent to her path.

"I have a job to do tonight," I hissed and looked around panicked.

What if he saw me like this? Say goodbye to my tip.

"Caroline is more of a dog than I originally thought," she said with a dark tone.

"I'm warning you," I hissed at her and tried to elbow her off but she caught it and twirled me so that I was facing her.

"I'm warning *you*, Jean," she said in slow enunciated words. "Your job tonight? *It's me.* I bought you. Now act like a good little escort and follow me into this goddamn museum before I lose my temper."

I was stuck between glaring at her and slapping her for her audacity which led to me just staring at her with my mouth open.

"That's right," she said and used my shocked state to turn me around and force me into the museum. The people guarding the door merely nodded to her as she passed. "You're my *bitch* tonight."

Shae

I wasn't *really* mad. Maybe just annoyed that she was late... but seeing the shock on her face when she realized the mess she was in was pure gold.

It took everything I had in me not to force her into the bathroom and tongue fuck her right there...but I had waited this long, and I could survive a few more hours. I didn't expect her to go home tonight; by the end of the night I planned to have her begging for me to take her back home where I would ravish her all night and into tomorrow morning.

I picked a Friday just because of that. So that there would be no excuse for her to leave. No work, no distractions, just me and her.

"I'm going to kill her," Jean muttered to herself. I let out a small laugh and reached over to pull out the clip that kept her hair up, causing her hair to fall around her in waves. It was much longer than it was three years ago. It fell to her mid-back and I could tell the ends had some leftover highlights in them.

"It looks better this way," I said and threw the contraption straight into the nearest trash can.

She let out a noise that she only did when I had offended her.

"What are you even doing?" she whispered as I pushed her into the elevator.

"We are here for an unveiling that I helped facilitate," I said simply and pulled her closer into me to inhale her scent. It was sweet, citrusy, and felt as though I had come home after a long trip. "And then after we will go to a house party."

"You only have me for two hours," she muttered against me not even trying to push me away.

This was too easy, I thought to myself. She had fallen right back into old habits even while her mouth spewed excuses.

Jean was way too focused on what other people thought about her, especially when she was doing her job. It's one of the things I loved about her. Not that she would hide her true self, or that she was a great actor...but knowing exactly how to make that mask crack was my specialty because I on the other hand, didn't give two fucks about what others thought about me.

Even her. I told her the other night that she was mine and little did she know what trouble awaited her once we reached that house party. There would be no going back from this, and I firmly expected her to come running back into my arms. She liked to play this big bad independent woman, but I knew how much she loved it when I came in and took control.

"Not true," I whispered in her ear letting my hand brush her lower back. I felt her shiver against my touch. "Caroline called. Said you requested more hours. We have all night, love."

Only then did she push away from me with a glare. *There it is.* The fight I had been waiting for.

As soon as the elevator dinged her mask was back on and this time it was her who pulled me out of the small metal box. When she threaded her small fingers through mine, I swore for the first time in three years my heart sped up.

"Don't think you are getting anything tonight," she warned. "That's not how this works."

"I know I won't get any," I said in a smug tone. *But you will be.*

Oh, the *plans* I had. They made my mouth water.

I removed my hand from hers and settled for an arm around her shoulders. She let me guide her to the newest arrival to the museum without so much as a protest, but I could feel the anger in her simmering underneath her skin.

This was one of the bigger unveilings I had helped with. People from all the most influential businesses groups were here to network with my partner, and myself...but I wasn't known for talking at these things and I would like to keep it that way and just focus on the person at my side.

Through the crowd I spotted my partner, Alvaro. I had been working with him for the past few years and while he liked to keep his art dealings *mostly* legal, he was willing to dabble in the more *exciting* things every once in a while behind closed doors.

"Shae," Alvaro said with a wide grin as he spotted me and Jean heading his way. He posed as the museum's most wealthy donor and has a knack for weaseling his way into business dealings that usually had nothing to do with him, but somehow he would always get the longer end of the stick.

"So glad you can make it. Who's this lovely lady?"

"This is Jean." I cut her off before she could give her escort name. She faltered a second before reaching out her hand to Alvaro and he promptly left a wet kiss on her knuckles. "Jean, Alvaro... He's throwing a party later that we are invited to."

Alvaro's brown eyes shined with delight at the mention of the party. He had cleaned up today with a freshly trimmed beard and a suede suit. Though with one look at the way his clothes stretched... I knew he was constricted by ropes under his clothing. He had a thing for being bound and whipped by women...not that I would judge. It was fun to watch.

"Jean, what a beautiful name. I can't wait to show you what we have in store tonight," he said with a chuckle.

I leaned down and tucked her hair behind her ear, making a show of my lips brushing her lobe.

"Do you see anything odd about his clothing?" I asked.

As if Alvaro knew what I was referencing, he ran his hand across his chest, showing that there was something underneath his clothing. His gaze darkened and his tongue swiped across his lips.

Jean gasped and a light blush immediately coated her cheeks. Her fingernails dug into my arm. While we hadn't tried *that* type of bonding before it would seem that she wasn't all that against it.

Interesting.

I nodded towards Alvaro, and he left us with a small wink.

"Is that...what you are into now?" she asked in a small voice. I felt her shiver against me and almost groaned aloud.

"Don't tell me you forgot when I tied you to the headboard," I said teasingly.

Her blush intensified.

"But *that's different*," she said.

"Do you want to try?" I asked. Her lashes fluttered when she looked up at me; there was an innocence to her eyes that made my inner beast ravenous.

"I—" Her voice dropped off when her eyes shifted to someone across the room. In an instant the blood drained from her face and that slightly aroused look turned into terror. "Shit, hide me."

I pulled her to my chest and turned, trying to locate what caused her to panic. There was a small crowd, but I picked out one couple in particular that looked a bit out of place. They were older and the woman was dressed in a far too conservative dress for this event and the type of people that normally came to these functions.

Alvaro never invited anyone that wasn't worth connecting with, at least in a business sense, so my curiosity rose.

Was this who she was hiding from?

"Who are we hiding from?" I asked even though I already had a feeling.

She pushed her face further into my open chest. I could feel the brush of her lips against me as she spoke.

"Get me to the bathroom and I'll tell you," she demanded.

A smile played at my lips.

"Or maybe I turn you around and show them who you really are," I suggested. "An old client? A coworker?"

"Shae, I swear to god," Jean hissed as I pulled myself away from her, but she pulled me back burying her face in my chest again. I didn't tell her just how close she was to exposing me, or how good her lips felt against me, especially as she licked them nervously.

"What do I get out of it?" I asked looking around again. The couple I assumed was the one she was hiding from had already left, but I could use this to my advantage, so I didn't bother to tell her.

"Shae," she warned.

"Your choice." I shrugged.

"I'll— Jesus. I'll give you a kiss," she said pathetically.

"More," I demanded and gripped at her hair forcing her to look at me. "Let me touch you."

"No," she choked out. "A kiss and I will continue to let you buy me for the night. If not, I will leave Caroline's shop."

"Then trade your kiss for a favor. One favor of my choice."

She let out a groan.

"Okay, but it can't involve you touching me."

Her tone told me this was her last straw.

"Fine," I said. "We will leave for Alvaro's early. I'm sure his girlfriend has already started without us."

I turned us back to the elevator and rushed us out of the place, but Jean did not relax until we were safely outside and a car was coming to pick us up. I let her stew in her own nervousness as we waited, enjoying the way she gripped onto me for dear life. Her breath against my bare skin was making me impatient and all I wanted to do was throw her into the surprise that I had waiting for her.

When the black SUV finally pulled up I let her jump in first before I followed her with giddiness threatening to explode inside me.

"So, who was it?" I asked after we had pulled away from the museum.

Her eyes fixed on the floor of the car.

"No one," she muttered.

"Doesn't seem like no one," I fought back. She didn't respond after that.

I leaned close and put my hand on her thigh, forcing my fingers between her legs. She let out a gasp and sent me a glare.

"I don't want to talk about it," she growled. "If you want to know so bad use your *favor*."

I let my fingers lightly trace her jaw, watching as her pupils expanded.

"I will use my favor for something *more interesting*," I purred.

"You can't touch me," she reminded.

"I won't have to use my favor for that," I said with a chuckle and moved back to the other side of the car.

"No fucking way," Jean hissed as I pulled her into Alvaro's house. Well...it wasn't the house he used for living but just one of the many ones he used to throw parties just like this.

"This is my night remember, I still have you for a few more hours," I reminded and pushed her through the entrance. Music was coming at us from all sides and as soon as you stepped in you were greeted by a completely naked woman holding a bowl of condoms and various other sex toys.

"Shae," Alvaro's girlfriend, Jenny, greeted with a smile. "I see you finally brought a guest. Are we participating tonight?"

I sent her a smile back and held onto Jean.

"Nope, but we will definitely be watching," I said.

"Well let me know if you need anything," she said with a sweet smile and gestured for us to go further in.

"Why did you think this was okay?" Jean hissed and pushed

me away from her. Her eyes were alight with fire, and she was so mad she was shaking.

"You needed to let loose a little," I said innocently. "You seem a little *tense.*"

She huffed but her attention was called, as soon as we stepped into the first room, by a couple fucking against the wall. The girl's moans were loud and the man was going at a positively ravenous pace. There were a few people that surrounded them all in their own stages of arousal. A couple with the man holding her from behind while his fingers were shoved in her pants, her head lolled back as she let out a moan. There were two girls to the side also watching for just a moment before they turned to another to start a heavy make-out session.

It was chaos in its own perfect way and it was just what Jean would need. She needed to be uncomfortable. She needed to be caught off guard. Or else she would just deflect until I was blue in the face.

"I want to leave," she said in an angry whisper to me.

"No, you don't," I said with a smile. "The old you would have loved this."

She was getting close to yelling; I could see her grind her teeth together and her hands ball into fists.

"I'm not her anymore," she said. I rolled my eyes and pushed her towards the kitchen, already knowing what awaited us. I had been here many times before but never have I had this much fun before. Her presence alone was already doing things to me. From the moment I saw her in the dress I bought, my underwear felt uncomfortably damp.

She stopped in her tracks when we entered the kitchen. There was a girl splayed on her back as she positively screamed in plea-sure while another woman licked the length of her pussy. The woman, who was very enthusiastic about her meal, was being rammed into from behind by a man that didn't even look up at us.

I smiled and pushed her towards the other end of the kitchen to pour us both a glass of whiskey as if it were my own home. Alvaro had all the houses set up the same and insisted that whoever joined take anything they wanted. This would be the first night that I did just that. Jean's eyes were still fixated on the group as I handed her the drink. She looked back to me wide-eyed and mouth open, the blush already back on her cheeks.

She took the glass and knocked it back without hesitation. I let out a laugh at the way her face contorted and handed her the next one. This one she was content with just sipping as her eyes shifted back to the group. I poured another but fully intended on holding it for her until she was ready for another.

She shifted as the girl in between the two threw her head back and wept as she climaxed. The man behind her did not stop in his ministrations, causing her cries to get louder the longer he went on.

"God damn..." she muttered. I let out a snort and her eyes snapped back to mine finally.

"Looks like it's been a while since you had one of those," I said playfully. I didn't mean it to have any weight but the way her face fell made my insides flutter. "Tell me who those people were?"

She let out a sigh and finished her glass with another pinched expression.

"You're gonna be wasted by the time I drag you out of here," I said with a pout.

"That's the point," she replied and reached for my glass, but I pulled it back, setting it on the counter. She sent me a glare. "My boyfriend's parents."

My breath caught in my throat, and I felt like a knife had stabbed me in the chest. *A boyfriend? Really?* I had promised myself this time that I wouldn't stalk her like I had in the beginning. I would wait for her to come to me and then I would start my plans...so hearing she had a *boyfriend* was painful news to me.

How dare she? While I waited this whole time for her? My pain quickly turned into anger, and I grabbed hold of her neck and forced her to me.

"You left out that detail," I hissed at her. "Have you been fucking around on me?"

She squirmed but could not release herself from my grip.

"We are broken up," she insisted.

I swallowed thickly and searched her eyes before pushing her away. The plans would have to be sped up. A *boyfriend* would be an unwanted distraction and would only further complicate everything.

Fuck it, I thought and downed my glass, putting the empty one on the counter next to me.

If this was what she wanted, this was how we would do it.

"I'm calling in my favor," I hissed and reached into my jacket pocket to pull out a small black toy.

"No," she whispered but her eyes screamed yes.

"Open your legs and I'll put it in if you find yourself so incapable," I hissed at her.

"You are not supposed to touch me," she said. "I have a boyfriend."

I pulled her closer and moved my hand from her neck to grip her hair and force her head back. She let out a groan but didn't move to stop me; instead she remained limp against me.

She knows her place.

I reached down between her legs with the toy, teasing her over her underwear.

"If you use the safe word I'll stop," I whispered against her lips. "You remember it right?"

She let out a shaky breath and her mouth opened as if to speak, but I beat her to it. In seconds I pushed aside her panties and shoved the bullet inside of her, but I didn't stop there. I pushed my fingers inside of her forcing it deeper. She was already so wet and squeezed around me as I pushed the toy.

Her deep moan pushed me further, but I stopped myself

before I could go any further. This would be punishment for going behind my back without remorse. I couldn't believe I had waited for her to come back, like an obedient puppy, and here she was fucking some other dude.

"Shae, we can't do this," she whispered against me. "And there are people here."

"We are here to watch," I growled at her. "Or at least I am. You on the other hand will sit still and keep that thing in you until I say so. That's my *favor* and I am calling it."

"Shae I'm serious, my boyfrien—" she whispered in a hushed tone.

"Don't you dare bring him up ever again," I hissed. "I don't want to hear about some two-pump frat boy that can't get you off. If you are so worried about it, take it out."

She paused for a moment and rubbed her thighs together, feeling the toy that rested deep inside her. She did not answer.

"Good," I said and leaned back. I was still fuming but I would get my revenge in a matter of minutes. Pulling out my phone I went to the toy's app and sent her a smirk before turning it on to the highest setting.

With a gasp she bolted forward and buried herself in my chest, clinging to the thin fabric of my shirt.

"Shae, not with so many people," she whispered against me. She couldn't hide her moans and the group that was fucking on the table looked over to us hesitantly. I shook my head and without another word they filed out of the kitchen.

This was why I liked his houses. He only chose people he knew he could trust and who respected boundaries.

"No one is watching you, love," I said and kept my hands at my side as she desperately clung to me.

This was the part where I would make her come to me... This was as far as I would allow myself to go tonight and if she made it through this...then I would see her next time and try it all over again.

She sent out a string of curses. I shifted against the counter letting my elbows hold me up and bent my knee out. I didn't even have to push the poor little thing; she swung her leg over mine and ground down on my knee with small whimpers spilling out of her mouth.

"Wow you really haven't come in a long time, huh?" I asked, mocking her.

"Shut up, I hate you so fucking much," she hissed against me and froze as her orgasm ran through her. She threw her head back and locked eyes with me as she came undone. I smiled at her and in return she glared at me.

"Don't get mad at me," I said. "I didn't even touch you. You can go home to your pretty little boyfriend with a free conscience. I mean it's essentially masturbation is it not?"

"You know damn well it's not," she hissed. "Turn it off."

"Nope," I said popping the 'p'. "You get what you get. Don't lie and say you aren't enjoying it. If anything, the danger of him finding out should excite you."

"Oh god," she moaned and rode my knee. "I'm going to fucking kill you after this."

I hummed and watched her dress ride up even further.

The whimpers began to fill the room and people started peeking through the door. Finally, I saw Alvaro show his face. I pushed Jean's face into my chest and held up a finger to him signaling to give me a minute. He gave me a devilish grin.

"Do ride your other client's knee as well as you do mine?" I teased but didn't move as she shuddered against me.

"I don't do that kind of work." She was still trying to hold onto her angry tone, but her whimpers made it obvious that she was about to come, *again*.

"Really?" I said in mock surprise. "You really should reconsider it as a career path."

Just as her body went taut I lowered the intensity on my phone to almost nothing. The glare I was met with took my breath away. She was even more of a spitfire than she was back then; by now she would have been begging me to touch her, but she simply just removed herself from me and straightened her dress.

She peered to the door just in time to see Alvaro walk towards us.

"I see you already got the party started," Alvaro said with a smile. He had taken his shirt off to show the intricate knots that ran down his arms and torso.

"Will you perform soon?" I asked and poured another drink for myself. I tried to hide my shaking hands but couldn't from Alvaro's sharp gaze.

"In just a few moments," he confirmed. "Did you want to partake?"

I could feel Jean's glare but I shook my head at him.

"A box would be nice though," I said and took a sip of the whiskey.

Alvaro let out a small chuckle.

"Box three has your name on it," he said and with a wave he left. Others started filling the kitchen and before Jean could protest I pushed her along to where the real fun awaited us.

Alvaro and his girlfriend had built this business with all types of people in mind. For those who like to watch, or be watched, the front of the house is great for that. Many never even look at the back and just stay in the front where they feel comfortable. In the back is where the real party starts and where people try some really freaky things.

For people like Jean though, she hates to be watched so near the back in the boxes would be preferable. Alvaro gutted the house and towards the back of the room where the living room and some spare rooms should have been, was a black stage that stood a few feet above the ground giving everyone a great view of what was to come. Toward the back and on the sides of the room there were rooms hidden by blacked-out windows for those who wanted more privacy but wanted to watch as well.

And behind those windows? Well, that's where I was taking Jean.

We could stay and watch inside the stage room like many did but I wanted to have her alone. It was the best way to get her defenses down.

I still couldn't get over the fact that she had a boyfriend. *A boyfriend.* If anything, I thought she would go for another woman...but she had settled for a boy. Quite frankly, I was insulted. We had one fight causing her to throw this huge fit and now she had even gotten herself a boyfriend.

Her eyes lingered on the stage as Alvaro's girlfriend and her assistants began setting up the bar that Alvaro would soon be bent over, but I quickly steered her to the glass with an etched number three in it. She gasped when I opened the door.

"Shae," she warned.

"For the last time Jean," I said annoyed by her constant panic. "I won't touch you until you ask me to."

I pushed her into the room and closed the door behind us. Rooms one, two, and three all had the same setup. A small bed in the corner, a chair in the middle of the room, and a counter on the far right filled with sex toys and water.

I grabbed her a water bottle and sat down on the chair in the middle of the room sipping my whiskey. She looked around awkwardly and opened the water bottle to take a big gulp.

"Nervous?" I asked her, noticing the shake in her hands.

She rolled her eyes at me.

"I know your games, Shae," she said with a huff. "I should have realized you'd play dirty when I saw you at the gallery."

"And yet you stayed," I murmured and rubbed the phone between my fingers ready to watch her squirm.

"I need the money," she said and cast her eyes downward.

"Little boyfriend can't help with that?" I asked.

"I don't want his money," she hissed.

"But you will take mine," I said and stood. "It must be serious if you are back to escorting."

I wanted to offer her the money, offer her anything. I would give her what she asked in a heartbeat but I was still angry...and she needed to pay for that.

She turned and looked at the stage. Alvaro was stripping his pants to reveal that he had no underwear underneath. The ropes were wrapped around his balls tightly and pulled at them when he stood straight up. He was already painfully erect and when his hand came to pump himself his girlfriend slapped his ass with a riding crop.

"I didn't know he was into *this stuff*," she murmured against the bottle.

"He's a big guy in the arts scene," I explained. "Even bigger in the BDSM sex club scene. He has houses like this all over the country. Last time I checked he was also opening a club in France."

This got her attention and instead of anger, when she looked at me her face was filled with curiosity.

"You know I still hate you right?" she asked catching me off guard. "The money, the sex toy, everything is just going to make that worse. You know that, right?"

I sent her a smile.

"We will see about that," I said. "Maybe you will feel so guilty about what we did here that you'll come running back."

She shook her head.

"We have a life," she said in an even tone. "He's a good guy, sweet, caring and he wants to be with me for a long time. It's serious."

If she really liked this guy she probably would be crying, but her eyes shot right back to Alvaro as he let out a deep moan, her boyfriend somehow not as important. They had him strapped to the bar, ass in the air and his girlfriend was already preparing his hole for the dildo she kept in her hand.

I pushed her closer to the window. Luckily the rooms were just a few feet higher than the ground of the stage floor so we were able to easily see over the crowd of naked bodies that were filling the room. I got her as close to the window as I could without her touching it. I positioned myself behind her, close enough to feel body heat and my breath on her neck but not enough to touch.

Without warning I turned the toy on again.

She let out a cry and leaned forward to brace herself on the cool window. I put my arms on either side of her and leaned to whisper in her ear.

"Let the show begin."

This was bad. *Really bad.* And so wrong.

I couldn't believe I was doing this right now. I should pull out that fucking vibrator and march out of this never to look back, but I couldn't force myself to.

And it had nothing to do with the money.

Even as the words traveled through my head, telling me to end it. Telling me to put a stop to this once and for all. I did not move and did not want to lose this feeling.

A part of me was excited about doing this again after so long. It was intoxicating to be around her; it always had been. She engulfed me with her being and caused me to lose all thought and will. I wanted her, wanted this much more than I had previously believed.

She was leaning over me; her breath was hot on my neck and her scent invaded my senses. I was surrounded by her, yet she refused to touch me. I wished that she would finally touch me. Just to take the decision out of my hands and put me out of my misery.

I stared wide-eyed at the stage, but it wasn't what held my attention anymore. I could hear the sounds of the people in the room and see them partaking in their own activities, but it was but an annoying buzz compared to the rush of blood in my ears. Instead, I hyper-focused on the shifting of Shae behind me, the movement of her hands to hover next to mine on the glass. I leaned my forehead against the cool glass, hissing as it touched my skin.

"Lost your fight?" she asked from behind me and gave a deep chuckle.

My lost orgasm was coming up on me fast and I shook against the window whimpering as I felt myself clench around the toy. I threw my head back as my orgasm ripped through me. It landed on Shae's chest and her eyes stared into mine as I shook beneath her.

"You're horrible," I said and shuddered as the vibrator kept up its pace. I could barely stand anymore, and I was sagging against her front. The vibrator was going at a pace stronger than I had ever used on myself, and it had been on this since I was able to sneak some time with a vibrator while Hunter was still around. I was severely out of practice, and it was showing.

I was embarrassed, ashamed of being so easily brought to the edge and I knew that if I peeked under my clothing, I would be mortified by the mess I was making.

"That I can admit to," she said with a smirk. "I can't believe you think a *little boy* can replace me."

Panic clawed at my throat. She didn't know him did she?

"I moved on, that's all," I said and let out an unconvincing whimper when she pushed me back onto the window forcing space between us.

"Then you have nothing to worry about," she said in a sly voice. I felt her hand tug at the zipper of my dress.

"That's too far," I hissed but my protest was cut off short when she unzipped me in one motion. I was shaking violently now and could barely hold up the fabric as it slid to the floor.

"Holy shit," she said from behind me and stepped back. "You're dripping all over."

Her chuckle filled the room and was so dark I couldn't help but flinch,

She pushed herself close to me again, her lips just barely touching my ear.

"You remember when I fucked you against the glass back at the penthouse?" she said, her arm coming in front of me like she was going to wrap it around me but instead her hand ghosted my stomach. Then slowly her hand trailed up to my breast all without touching it, but I swear I could feel the heat radiating off of it. "It was just like this except everyone could see you as I rammed that dildo so far up that greedy pussy of yours that your screams shook the glass."

Jesus Christ. Her words alone were about to make me come.

I wanted her to so badly close the distance between us. Being in between her and the window like this, her scent invading my senses, it was all too much for me to handle.

My whole body flushed at her words but before I could turn around and yell at her the vibrator stopped. A low whine made its way out of my mouth.

I turned to see her back to me as she walked to the chair. She plopped down in it and spread her legs, adjusting herself much like she did the night last week. Her eyes drank in my form hungrily, but she didn't say anything, instead just left me in that spot bare except for my bra, panties, and heels.

"What is the point of all this?" I asked with a growl. Her eyes widened when I reached in between my legs and pulled out the bullet. I could barely hold in the moan as my fingers brushed my swollen neglected clit.

She patted her lap and looked at me expectantly.

"I'm not sitting on you," I said in a growl.

"There is only one chair," she said with a smirk. "And they only just started. I paid for at least two more hours so if you want to stand those two hours be my guest."

My eyes shifted to the bed in the corner. It seemed like a

better option than the chair. The blankets were black, and it looked like it was clean enough.

"I wouldn't suggest that," she said. "I'm hanging on by a thread and my patience is wearing thin. Come here."

I swallowed at the tone of her voice. It excited me and scared me at the same time. With a deep breath I stepped out of my dress and walked slowly to her. When I stopped in between her legs she raised her hands as if to show me she wasn't a threat. I looked at her critically for what felt like the first time that night. Her shirt was wrinkling, and her pants were already starting to stain. Besides that, she looked as put together as she had been at the museum. With stiff movements I sat on her lap. Something bulged against my ass, and I quickly realized that she had come strapped. She had really thought she would have her way with me tonight.

I cursed internally. *How the hell did I not realize this before?* A thrum of desire made its way through me.

She shifted against me and placed her chin on my shoulder.

"Take off your bra," she commanded and gripped the sides of the chair.

"This is too far, I told you," I hissed at her. "You get me to accompany you tonight and that's it."

"You weren't complaining earlier when you were riding my knee," she whispered in my ear. She nipped at my lobe, and I let out a shaky breath. "Or while you came around that toy."

"Shae," I warned.

"If I didn't know any better"—she paused to let out a breathy chuckle—"it would seem that this whole situation turns you on. Here you are pretending that you're such a *good little girlfriend* while you're ready to bend over for me."

I swallowed my guilt.

"I wouldn't fuck you," I lied. "I am here for the money, and you know it."

There was a moment of silence that passed through us. I

could hear her hands grip the chair, strong enough to make the leather squeak in protest.

"You lie so sweetly," she said in a purr. Her right hand left the chair to cup my wet core. I couldn't help the moan that left my lips or the jerk of my hip.

Please. Please. Please. Please. My thoughts begged for her to take me, going against everything I was supposed to do.

When her hand disappeared, I sagged against her chest. The heaving of her chest did not go unnoticed by me.

"Tell me something real, my love," she said in a husky voice. "Something no one else knows." My brain froze. What was this? What was she getting at?

"What?" I asked confused by her change in tactic.

"You heard me," she grumbled.

"I—" I stopped when the first thought came to my mind. But before I backed down I let the words fall from my lips. "I love him."

You could hear a pin drop.

"More than you love me?" she asked, her voice unwavering.

The thought that came to mind was so violent, so heart-breaking I couldn't breathe.

"I love you, Shae," I told her, tears in my eyes. I was begging her, pleading with my eyes for her to say it back. She looked up at me through her dark lashes with a blank expression.

"Does that make you feel better about what's going on here?" she asked. "If so, by all means go on but I don't want to have to tell you again—that's not what's going on here. I will never love you back."

This was too much; I should have left as soon as we walked in the door. This was the game she played. She would toy with me knowing I couldn't resist her then throw it right back in my face. I had no idea what I was going to tell Hunter, nor did I know how I was going to look at him after this.

This was how it always was with her. I would bend to her will and never look back. I had lost many friends since I was with her, just getting too tangled in her that I forgot myself wholly. The way she commanded my body, the way she took care of me, it was all too much to handle back then. That was until she hit my final straw. She asked me to do the *one thing* I couldn't, something that would make me really lose myself completely.

That thought alone snapped me out of my fog and I shot up. I hurried over to my dress and scrambled to put it on.

"You don't control me anymore," I said as I zipped my dress.

"Leave and you won't get the money," she threatened. Her voice was hard and when I met her eyes her face was stone cold.

She didn't like losing.

"It's not worth this," I said. "I have a life without you, and I would like to keep it that way. Don't call Caroline and do not request me again."

"I will do what I want," she said with a growl. Her knuckles turned white as she gripped the chair. "If I want to request you, I will. If I want to fuck you I will. Don't test me, Jean."

"*Don't test me Jean,*" I said in a mocking tone and sent her a glare. "I will also do what I want and will quit the escorting if you insist on requesting me. And *no,* you will not fuck me. I have a boyfriend for that, and it would do you good to remember that."

There was a tense silence as she stared at me, breathing heavily.

This was my fault, I thought to myself.

I knew who she was, and I still let her push me around like this. But I wasn't the girl I once was, I knew that. Now she needed to understand that too.

"Keep your dirty money," I said and with a flip of my hair I left the room.

WHEN I ENTERED my house that night I was grateful that Hunter was already asleep. My hair was a mess and I had cried in the Uber on the way over here. He would worry like the good boyfriend he was, and I would be forced to swallow my guilt as I tried to act like nothing happened. I let the dress fall to the floor and decided to throw away my panties entirely. They were still wet, and I knew that even if I washed them I would be reminded of the way Shae's fingers invaded me.

I won't touch you, she had said.... What utter *bullshit.* She was a master manipulator and knew exactly where my faults were. She played me like an instrument and the worst part was that I wanted her to. I loved the way it felt when she held me. Loved the way her voice sent shivers down my spine.

I didn't realize just how much my body ached for her until she stood over me and refused to touch me. I craved her, even so many years later. It was stupid and *unfair.*

"Jean?" Hunter's sleep-filled voice came from the bed. Even though it was dark I wiped my face in case he saw my makeup running. I discarded my bra and heels and climbed into bed with him.

"Hey, sorry to wake you," I said in a soft voice.

He pulled me to him immediately and froze when his hand passed my bare ass.

"You always surprise me when you come home late from drinking," he said in a deep voice. There was a slight chuckle to his tone, but it only made my stomach twist painfully.

"Gotta keep things lively," I joked, not at all feeling in a joking mood. "I'm excited for the surprise tomorrow."

"You'll love it," he said as his hand dipped lower and lower.

I gasped as his fingers found and ran between my folds.

"Hunter we don't have—"

He shushed me.

"Turn around," he said and helped me flip so I was lying on my side while facing the door and pulled me flush against his front. I could feel his erection against me, but he didn't move to pull it out, instead he just plunged two fingers deep inside me.

"Yes," I moaned and threw my head back against him. The fullness of his fingers caused me to shudder. I had been on edge all night; even after the multiple orgasms I still felt something was missing.

He pumped into me slowly. The sounds of his fingers moving in my wetness filled the room and caused my nipples to tighten. I moved to pinch them, needing the extra stimulation. He let out a grunt and removed his fingers just to pull his erection out. He wasted no time in finding my entrance and shoving himself deep inside me. I let out a deep moan and hooked my leg over his to allow him deeper access.

"Fuck this feels so good," he groaned against my neck and started to thrust into me. I knew he wouldn't last long, he never did, so I reached between my legs and rubbed hard circles on my clit.

"Faster, Hunter," I said with a gasp as I felt jolts of pleasure ride through me.

He obliged and began pushing into me faster, whispering and groaning in my ear, but when I closed my eyes to enjoy it my mind still wandered back to Shae.

I imagined it was her behind me, fucking me with no mercy while she assaulted my clit. She wouldn't be as gentle as he was and she sure as hell wouldn't be telling me how good I felt. She would laugh, tell me how needy I was. Degrade me in ways Hunter would never think to...and it would turn me on, make me even wetter than before.

"Look at how much of a whore you are," she would say as she pinched my clit, causing me to scream. "So obedient. So wanton. Tell me how much you like it when I fuck you."

There had been many a time where she would deny me an orgasm until I was screaming her name. Those were my most powerful ones, the ones I remembered the most clearly...but that was not the image that helped me come tonight.

The image that threw me over the edge just as Hunter was about to finish was her waking me in the mornings as she whispered the sweetest things into my ears. It was the moment she told me she loved me for the first and last time.

I winced as Hunter pulled out of me.

"That was great, babe," Hunter said through pants.

"It was," I said with a dry mouth.

"I love you babe," he said and pulled me closer to him.

"Ya... Me too."

I DIDN'T SLEEP that night. I just stared at the darkness until little wisps of light shined through the room. It was quiet and allowed me to mull over just how much of a mess my life had become.

The insomnia was in part because of my guilt but also the overwhelming thought of how much money I would have to pay back. I had sold my car to pay off the loans six months ago and the only other thing that was in my name...was this apartment. So, if I didn't figure out something soon both Hunter and I would need a home and there would be no keeping my debt a secret.

As I rose at six in the morning I showered quickly and dressed in a sweatshirt and jeans. I chose to make breakfast for Hunter, or at least tried to. The only thing I could really cook is eggs and that left much to be desired. But it was the least I could do after his literal bending over backwards for me the last few weeks.

Peeking back at a sleeping Hunter I was that he was still deep asleep and wrapped in the covers. He looked even more boyish now with his hair sticking up at all angles and the cover clutched tightly to his face. I closed the door to the bedroom and quickly made a call to Caroline.

"Jesus Christ it's six in the fu—"

"I quit," I said cutting her off. "You fucked up Caroline, this was my last straw."

"No, no, no, no wait a minute." Her voice sounded much more awake than before. "I'm sorry Jean, she was paying a lot of money and said that she would take you to the museum. I didn't think it would be that bad."

"She dragged me to a sex party," I hissed in a low voice and prepared toast. "It's highly unprofessional and I am done with her." I paused for a moment. "And you. Wire the money to my account and this will be the last time we talk."

She tried to say something, but I hung up on her, not willing to budge on this. It was a stupid idea to get back into this business; I had foolishly thought that I could make a few thousand dollars and pay off the immediate loans while juggling my full-time gig all while keeping it from Hunter... It was just a matter of time before he would have found out. It's better this way, at least I can stop him from ever having to realize what I was doing.

Hunter chose that moment to shuffle into the kitchen with a sleepy grin.

"Breakfast?" he asked in an excited tone.

"It's just eggs," I said and sat down at the bar.

"Made by you," he said with a smile and took his place beside me. "Which makes them all the more delicious."

He took an exaggerated bite. I took a small hesitant one and was surprised when I realized they weren't half bad.

"So, what are we doing today?" I asked. He rolled his eyes and let out a laugh.

"So impatient," he teased. "We are going to a wreck-it room so we can break a bunch of shit until you feel better."

My heart melted at his thought. *All this because he caught me crying?*

My happy moment was ruined by Caroline's name flashing across my screen. With a huff I declined her message. Hunter gave me a look.

"She messed up last night," I said honestly. He nodded.

"Well, I hope you can work it out," he trailed off. "But if not, you can imagine her at the end of the bat."

I let out a laugh.

"That sounds nice," I said.

And it did. Suddenly a life with this man didn't seem half

bad...as long as I could keep the others away I'm sure I could be happy here with him.

❧

THE WRECK it room was the best thing I had done in my life. Hunter was content to stand outside and watch as I totally destroyed a room full of broken computers, chairs... I even got to smash a vase.

I had never thought of myself as a violent person, and I very rarely got so angry that I had to let out some steam...but the experience was positively therapeutic. I laughed loudly as pieces of wood and metal shattered in the air. Hunter cheered me on from outside and I, at times, even found myself cheering along with him. When my thirty minutes was up I was panting and sweat dripped down my back. I ripped off the bulky glasses and tugged off the protective suit as soon as I left the room.

"That was the best thing I have ever done!" I squealed to Hunter. As soon as I could detangle myself from the protective suit, I jumped into his arms. "Thank you!"

He chuckled and planted a kiss on my forehead.

"I'm glad you feel better," he said. "Let's go get some lunch?"

I nodded and got my stuff only to be interrupted by a phone call from Caroline *again.* Hunter spotted and gave me a sympathy smile.

"Take it," he said. "I'll go finish up front."

I nodded and waited until he turned the corner to answer.

"Fuck off Caroline," I hissed.

"It's me," Shae said from the other line.

My heart jumped into my throat, and I quickly looked down the hall to make sure Hunter wasn't coming back.

This was dangerous, my mind told me. *But exciting.*

"Even worse," I said. "Don't call me. Both of you leave me alone."

"Ten grand," she said.

"What?" I hissed and threw my bag over my shoulder.

"I'll pay you ten grand to keep me company again," she explained. "This is my last offer though."

I paused. Ten grand would cover the late payments on the medical bills. They would stop hounding me. Stop hounding my father. Then I could keep the apartment with Hunter...

God, Hunter.

"No," I said quickly. "I know what you want, and you won't get it from me. Don't call me again."

"No touching, just a dinner," she said. I swallowed thickly.

"You lost your chance after last night," I said and finally hung up on her.

I walked to the front of the establishment and Hunter's smile was the first thing I noticed. Even though this was for the best I couldn't get past the anxiety gnawing at my stomach.

Jean

THREE YEARS EARLIER

"If I was into women," my mother said with a playful light in her eyes, "she would be my type."

I let out a scandalized gasp, playing along.

"Mother," I scolded. "You are a happily married woman."

She sent me a beaming smile showing all her teeth and causing the sides of her eyes to wrinkle.

She was a carefree woman, or at least she tried to be when I was growing up. I loved my mom. I had a less than savory relationship with my dad, but my mom was always there for me. Even when I had my rebellious teenage years, my mom was there with me through it.

I remember a time when I came home absolutely wasted at seventeen and instead of yelling at me, she simply tucked me into bed and made me promise that if this ever happened again that I would call her before trying to sneak back in.

She always tried to look after me, but as I got older I realized that I needed to take care of her as well. She was no longer the woman who was full of life and energy, she needed time to rest now, time to recuperate after being in the hot sun for too long. And even if dad couldn't find it in him to care about her, at least I would.

97

"That doesn't mean you can't look, Jean," she teased back.

She looked over at us with a small smile before bringing us a tray of drinks. I was surprised that she was even flattering us both. I knew that she could do this with clients, but this was woefully and selflessly doting on us.

It warmed my heart. It made me feel like we were more than the facade that we wore in public. That we were the doting couple that I dreamed we could be.

"I am flattered Joanna," Shae said with a smirk. "Here is your lemon water, Jean your Long Island, and my deliciously simple whiskey."

Mom pouted when she took a sip of her water.

"Aw I was hoping you slipped a bit of vodka in here," she joked. "I was sadly disappointed."

I sent her a look.

"The doctor told you to go easy on the alcohol," I reminded.

Just like he told her to get more exercise, eat more greens, and overall take care of her body...but still she ignored them.

I used to come with her to the doctors, but lately she had thrown a fit when I tried to go and refused to let me in with her.

She rolled her eyes but leaned back in her chair anyways.

"Life is so short, Jean. Don't forget to live a little in between all your worrying," she said with a meaningful look.

The summer breeze kicked up just slightly and I sighed. We took my mom onto the open balcony to enjoy the view of New York. I hated the heights, but Shae had convinced me to come up here on multiple occasions just to show me that I wouldn't magically fall off the edge and after a while it started to scare me a bit less.

I sent her a grateful smile as I took a drink of my Long Island. She had met my mother in passing but this was the first time she invited her to the penthouse. Besides Caroline no one had been invited, even my father. She didn't like him even though she only saw him once; apparently that was enough for her.

"She's still very nervous in crowds," Shae commented. "And heights. It took me a while to convince her to come out here."

I rolled my eyes at her.

"Jean," mom scolded. "Look at how sweet she is to you. Drinks? Helping you get over your fears?"

She let out a light laugh.

"Mom, stop it," I said feeling my face flame.

"How long have you been together, again?" she asked.

"Eight months, *Mother*," I reminded for the third time today.

She nodded thoughtfully and took a sip of her water.

"You should be thinking of marriage." I choked on my drink. Shae reached over and patted my back.

"It's too soon for that," I hissed at her. My eyes shot over to Shae in a panic. She had a tense smile on her face. Marriage wasn't spoken about between us, hell she only just recently confessed her feelings for me and even that was brushed off as if it never happened.

Shae was not the type of person to do anything serious besides work. From the time I had spent with her I could tell that all she wanted was someone to stay by her side and nothing more.

"You should hold onto someone like her," Mom said but I wasn't sure if it was directed at me or Shae.

Jean

Caroline paid me a total of five thousand dollars for my services for the last two weeks and by Monday morning I had paid half of the late fees that were on the account. It was enough of a dent so that I could sleep at night but not enough for me to completely relax.

I was still five thousand dollars short, and I wouldn't get paid for another week. And even then I wouldn't have enough to pay for living and the late fees.

I got up early one day and sat at the bar with my laptop just staring at the pure chaos that was my mom's medical account. Even though I had paid the five thousand dollars, last month's interest payment went through, and it looked as though I barely made a dent in the total.

It made me almost regret cutting Caroline off. I knew Shae wouldn't give up...but maybe if I could just get a client? Maybe Gary?

"Jean," moaned Hunter from the other room. "It's so early."

I shut my computer before he could come into the room.

"We have to meet your parents for brunch you know," I reminded.

"But it's like 6 a.m.! On *Labor Day!*" he yelled, his voice muffled by the covers.

I let out a sigh.

I didn't want to go and be glared at by his parents...but I promised myself I would try, even if it made me uncomfortable. I needed to move on, *seriously* and this was the way to do it. This was what grown adults did...and now it was my turn to swallow my pride and make a better future for myself.

I got up from the bar to go check on Hunter. His head was barely peeking out of the covers and hair stuck up in all different ways just like it had every other morning. His eyes opened playfully and a smile big enough to show his dimples showed on his face. He lifted the covers, inviting me in.

I smile at the domesticity of it all.

I climbed into bed and pressed my cold nose into his warm, naked chest.

"Argh!" Hunter yelled and tried to push me away, but I just wrapped my arms around his torso and splayed my cold finger against his back. "You are the devil, woman."

I let out a laugh.

We stayed in bed cuddling until it was eight o'clock and then I really forced him out of bed. He left to shower with a kiss to my lips and a slap to my backside. I rolled my eyes at his antics and went to go pick out something acceptable for his parents.

It was getting just a bit warmer outside, so I chose a bright yellow sundress and some strappy sandals to go with it. It covered my shoulders and had a square neck with a cinch at the waist, so I was hoping that it would be conservative enough for his parents but also ensure that I would still not look too much like a nun.

I put my hair up in a twist and decided to forgo the makeup.

After years of doing what I did it was easy to get lost in the changes of your appearance. People paid me to look the way they needed me to and just the smallest change could drastically change the message you put out there. Some people asked for a pretend housewife, some asked for an irresistible girlfriend, but for

Hunter and his parents...they required something a bit more innocent.

So, we have a bright yellow dress, almost zero of my curves showed, no jewelry, and a fresh face. It should fit the image of the type of person Hunter should be with.

Hunter let out a low whistle when he came out of the bathroom. I turned to see him in nothing but a towel low on his waist.

"That sundress does something to me," he commented with a grin.

I rolled my eyes at him.

"Hurry up, last time with minimal traffic it took forty minutes but right now it's rush hour," I noted.

"We can be late," he said in a suggestive tone and came to hug me from behind. I was surprised to feel that his dick was already hard. I don't know why the sudden change in his arousal made me panic but I let out a nervous laugh and squirmed away from him.

"You can, I cannot," I said. "I still have your parents to impress, and I can't do that if we show up late. If anything, we need to be there earlier and set up."

Apparently his family hosted brunch and luncheons whenever they could and today just so happened to be that day, so we would be heading back to that fabulous-looking house and garden to enjoy some alcohol and finger food. It was the parties I hated the most. No one was drunk enough to let loose, and everyone was always in some sort of sour mood. It was easier when you were hidden by dim lighting and the loud chatter of a party.

"We have people for that," he said casually and dropped his towel. "Get over here."

WE WERE LATE. Or at least later than I wanted to be after Hunter dragged me back into bed. He got off fairly quickly, but I was left panting, wanting, and unable to catch up to his quick orgasm. I was annoyed to have to fix my hair and rumpled dress after I had spent time putting together the perfect ensemble. I really wasn't planning to show up to this party horny and unsatisfied as hell, but there we were.

Hunter squeezed my hand and sent me a smile... He must have felt my annoyance.

"Let's get some drinks in us," he teased and pushed me into the garden. There were just as many people as last time, but I felt much more prepared, and I was satisfied to see I was dressed correctly. Their sundresses were probably hundreds of dollars, but my thirty-dollar one that I had gotten on sale at the mall fit in perfectly. I felt a weight lift off my shoulder.

This would be okay, I thought. I *would be okay.*

He led me to one of the various waitstaff that had a tray full of mimosas. The waiter smiled at me as I took one off his tray. I smiled back and clicked my glass against Hunter's before taking a sip.

"We need some food, or this mimosa will be my last," I said with a small giggle. Hunter's eyes lit up and he waved down another waitstaff with a tray full of fruit.

This was the life Hunter was used to. He was a natural here and had become accustomed to ordering people around. Used to not having to want anything in life because he would always have it right at his fingertips.

I was envious and angry at the same time. How many times had I wished for this life? How many times during my young adult life was I left crying because I didn't know how I would have paid that month's rent?

He wasn't like me. Wasn't like Sha—

Hunter turned to me quickly and shoved a strawberry into my mouth, his fingertips lingering on my lips. I cocked my brow at him. *What has gotten into him?*

I didn't mind it per se... He was just usually more contained than this.

"They will serve bigger food later once people have had enough time to mingle," he said. "Networking and all that."

I nodded and let him continue to feed me sweetened fruit. It was enough for now and the more I sipped my mimosa the better I felt about being here. Maybe this wasn't so different from the parties I escorted before. At least while I had the drink in my hand, I felt invincible.

"Mother!" Hunter said excitedly and waved. I turned to see Mr. and Mrs. Williams walking over to us both with glasses in their hands. Immediately all my fuzzy, confident feelings sizzled out of me.

Invincible, I thought with a scoff. *Ya, right.*

"Jean, don't you look darling today," Mrs. Williams said in a light tone. "The yellow is so bright I didn't know how we missed your arrival."

I shut my jaw and plastered a sweet smile on my face.

"Mrs. Williams, thank you. Such a lovely party," I said not commenting on her insult.

"Jean wanted to get here early to help but I was lagging," Hunter said with a sheepish grin. "Isn't that sweet of her?"

Mr. Williams let out a huff and averted his eyes.

"That's a job for waitstaff," he commented.

There was an awkward tension in the air that weighed between us like a blanket.

"Did you do something like that previously?" Mrs. Williams asked, her tone still sweet. "Waiting?"

I felt a spike of anger run through me. *Jesus Christ, are these people for real?*

"He just told me that you two put on parties like this all the time so I thought that must be hard on you, wanted to see if we *young people* could take some weight off your shoulders..." I trailed and sipped my champagne. "But it looks like you handled that already."

"Very sweet," she commented her eyes narrowing.

There was a stare down between me and her and suddenly

everything clicked into place. I had seen mothers like her before, mostly on T.V. but here I got to see it in real life.

She was jealous of her son dating.

Ever since we had met she had given me this stare and now with all the backhanded compliments, it was far too predictable.

Disgusting.

Mr. Williams straightened and peered past us, breaking our staring contest. His bored expression was suddenly gone and in its place was a hungry look that caught me off guard. He pushed past us, and Mrs. Williams shook her head with disgust.

"I still don't get why he's so keen to work with *people* like that," she said with venom.

Both Hunter and I turned to see who it was, and I saw white spots in my vision and my knees threatened to give out. I clutched Hunter's shirt so that I wouldn't fall to the ground in a heap.

There in a casual button-up and light jeans was my living nightmare. Shae smiled widely at Mr. Williams as he approached. She was so out of place here it was almost laughable. While her clothing fit there was an aura around her that told everyone to stay away.

"Is she...?" Hunter asked in a whisper.

"Obviously," his mother replied with disgust. "But apparently she deals in arts and has contacts your father could use to expand to other continents."

I swallowed thickly at their words. I knew because of his upbringing that he and his parents would be hesitant around gay people but this... This was insane. What was even more insane was just how animated Mr. Williams was when talking to her.

What the fuck did she think she was doing?

Her eyes drifted to our group and a smile graced her face. This one was more sinister, and I knew it all too well. Mr. Williams looked over to us as well and moved to bring her over to us.

No.

This couldn't be happening. Was she really going to meet Hunter right now? The boyfriend she was poised to destroy? This couldn't be a coincidence. She wouldn't spill my job would she? Oh god, our relationship?

But really... How did she, in only three days, find out who Hunter's parents were and get herself invited here?

The fucking art gallery, I realized. I was the one who had given away their identity, *I'm so fucking stupid.*

Sweat coated my palms and I took a sip of my glass to stead myself only to find it empty. I quickly gave Hunter my glass and took his. He gave me a look but was quickly wiped away as Shae stood in front of us.

"Hunter right?" she asked with a grin. "Your father has told me all about you and insisted I come today to meet you." Her eyes shifted to mine. "And who is this ravishing lady?"

My cheeks went up in flames.

"Jean, my girlfriend," Hunter said in a curt tone. "It's nice to meet you. Jean and I were just about to get some more food."

He was ready to pull us away from the group, but his father stopped us and outright crushed any dream I had of escaping this hell.

"Actually, I was thinking you could talk a bit more with Shae," he said. "She can help in your dealings with our European vendor."

Hunter's Adam's apple bounced as he swallowed. Shae met his gaze with an easy smirk. She was goading him. She was only an inch or two shorter than him and while he stood straight and unwavering, she looked as though she was relaxed as ever.

Were they even in the same line of business? How did this even work? Anyone involved with Shae were straight-up gangsters or white-collar criminals... How was this hymn-singing, church-going family involved in any of that?

"Sounds great," he said. "Let's search out some food and a nice seat in the shade."

"Ah yes," she said and pushed her hand in her pockets. "Skin like that must burn easily. Such a caring boyfriend."

He didn't comment instead just sent me a smile and pulled us to a different side of the garden where there were less people and more seats. My chest felt tight, and I heard her walk behind us. I knew I shouldn't, but I peeked over my shoulder only to see her eyes hooded and her tongue swipe across her lips.

My breath caught and I quickly looked at the ground in front of us.

I was so fucked.

～

"Carter's a bitch for imports, use Jonson," she said with a firm tone. "Carter's greedy with his ports and loyalty means nothing to him."

"He taxed us an extra ten percent *on top* of his ridiculous fees," Hunter replied in an exacerbated tone. He took another swig of his fourth mimosa. If he didn't stop soon I would be dragging his body home.

After the initial awkwardness Hunter had easily hit it off with Shae...or at least the front she uses for business. I had seen her turn this switch one too many times and could see right through her plan.

"Like I told you, Jonson," she said with a smile. "I'll send you his information."

We were at a small iron table under a shaded tree. The rest of the party was far away from us, leaving us in complete privacy as we talked. Hunter had long ago put his hand on my upper thigh and the more he drank the higher it seemed to go. I didn't know if Shae could see but from the look she was giving me, she had to have guessed.

"My dad said you did something with art?" Hunter asked. She gave him a wicked grin.

"I wouldn't ask too much about that," she warned.

"Oh, come on," he egged on. Were his words slurring already? I watched as he rested his head on his palm, but it was unsteady.

"Hunter?" I asked hesitantly. "Are you okay?"

He gave me a look like I was crazy.

"I'm fine, babe," he replied.

"You look a little drunk, Hunter," Shae said, a smile still planted on her face. "Maybe we should go lie you down."

"Nah I'm good," he said and tried to get up but lost his balance. I shot up to stop him from falling.

Shae came over to the other side of him and put his arm over her shoulder. Her hand brushed my side and I recoiled.

"Why don't you be a good girl and go tell his parents he's going to take a nap in the living room," she said.

"Hey, don't talk to my girlfriend like that," Hunter protested, the slur in his speech more defined now.

"Oh, is she not a good girl, then?" she asked Hunter. He responded with a pout. "Ahh a bad girl then. Yes, she *does look* like one of those."

"Stop it," I hissed. "Hunter I'll go tell your mother."

She waved me off and lugged him to the back door. I sighed and went to go find Mrs. Williams. When I did I saw that she was already also a lot gigglier than before.

"Mrs. Williams," I called as I came to her side. Her smile dropped slightly when she saw me. "Hunter has drunk too much. He's going to sleep if off in the house."

She nodded and waved me off like she did one of her waitstaff. I didn't have time to worry about that, not when my ex was holding my boyfriend hostage and possibly whispering all my secrets to him.

I hurried into the house not even looking at the interior. It was huge, obviously, but the only thing in my mind was to find Hunter. I searched the first few rooms near the back door but there was no one.

My heart rate rose with each step and the panicked thoughts of this all blowing up in my face only got worse in my mind.

What would she say?

Would she tell him about us?

About the other night?

God… What would Hunter even say to that?

As I circled back and ran past one of the rooms near the front, I heard a loud moan fill the hallway. It was Hunter. I held my breath and opened the door to see Hunter passed out on a couch that was placed in the middle of the room. Stepping in I realized this was more of a sitting room than a bedroom and felt a bit better as the last time I was in a room with Shae… Well we all know what happened there. There was a couch under the window to the far left where Shae sat. There was a bookshelf on the other side of the room and a closet but besides that, the room was bare.

I gave her a look and moved to kneel in front of Hunter, feeling his head and checking his pulse.

"I didn't kill him, Jean," she said from behind me. I heard her get up from the chair but didn't pay her mind. "Just gave him a little something to relax. It'll wear off in a bit."

I heard her lock the door.

Ice cold panic pushed through my veins. I turned to stare at her wide-eyed.

"What the fuck do you think you are doing?" I hissed. "You drugged him? Are you trying to get caught?"

"Get caught? Why are you acting like these are people to fear? His mom is getting drunk out there because her husband's dick has dried up and flaunting around family made money because she is insecure about it," she said with a laugh. "I am not *scared* of him or his family, Jean."

"I am *scared* of losing the only semblance of normal in my life!" I yelled at her. "I have worked hard to get where I am now."

She rolled her eyes at me.

"You mean stuck in a shitty apartment and in debt?" she asked. "Your life sucks Jean. Don't lie to yourself."

My jaw dropped at the conviction in her words.

She didn't wait for my response, and it only took her three long strides to reach me. There was no smile on her face as she yanked me up by my arm and forced me to the other couch in the room. I fought her enough to get my feet on the ground, but she still forced herself in between my knees and kneeled before me.

"I warned you," she said in a dangerous tone. "I gave you a chance and you didn't take it. This is what you get. You will sit pretty and take what I give you, hell I expect you to thank when I am done."

"Shae this is crazy," I whispered and tried to kick her but she only used my momentum to pull my leg over her shoulder.

Her hands massaged my thighs and a fiery heat started to build in my belly. The way her gaze watched as even just a little movement set me alight was intoxicating as much as it was embarrassing.

There was no denying the tension that was quickly filling the air. As her hand got closer and closer to my now damp underwear I couldn't catch my breath, nor could I find It in me to push her away.

"Stay silent and your *boyfriend* won't wake up and see what a bad girl you really are," she growled, and her face disappeared between my skirt. I was too slow to push her away and her lips attacked my clothed core.

I panicked and looked towards Hunter. His face was still pointed towards us, but his eyes were closed. By the deep rise and fall of his chest I could tell that he was knocked out cold.

"Shae stop it," I hissed but I couldn't hide the gasp when her fingers pulled aside my underwear and her wet tongue met my folds. "*Ah fuck.* This is so wrong Shae, please."

Her response was to suck so hard on my clit that my back bowed.

"You like it," she said against me. "Maybe even more that we are doing it in front of him."

When she pushed two fingers into me her head reemerged, and her lips claimed mine. I stifled a moan as her fingers pounded into me. The silent room was filled with obscene wet sounds that only heightened my arousal.

Fuck, she's right, I thought as her thumb brushed my clit. *I loved the way she played with my body. Even in a situation like this my mind got lost in her touches.*

I kissed her back and tangled my hands in her hair. She grinned and chuckled against me like she had just won the sick game we were playing. She had a right to because she was winning. With each thrust of her hand, I found myself lost in her once again. Lost in the way she licked my bottom lip before biting it and bringing it into her mouth. Lost in the way she trapped my hips and stopped them from moving as they tried to desperately meet her pace.

When she pulled away again she only shot me a smirk before she ducked beneath my skirt again.

I moaned and pushed her head closer to where I needed it. She rewarded me by moving back to my clit and pulling it back into her mouth. The heat inside me was out of control, I could feel it start its journey outward from my belly and my body stiffened. My eyes darted to the couch again when Hunter shifted but he merely turned and faced away from us, still sleeping.

I couldn't hold it in anymore. I so desperately tried to hold myself together but even after so long, Shae knew my body better than I did and the heat exploded within me pulling a loud cry from my mouth.

I continued to shudder violently as I came but that didn't stop Sha's assault on my clit winding me up even further.

"Fuck, Shae please I can't—"

I couldn't stop the groan as she continued to suck.

"Please what, love?" she said against my folds. This time she slipped three fingers inside me easily. "Are you asking me to fuck you, right here on this couch? You know I always come strapped."

"No," I said quickly, but my insides were screaming *yes*. My hips bucked as her hand found a rhythm once more. She leaned back to look at me, her hair disheveled, and her lips wet with my release. I couldn't even finish my protests as she pinched my clit.

I threw my head back and slammed my hand over my mouth.

I couldn't help it as my hips met her movements, by this time it was like I was fucking her hand.

"Look at you," Shae whispered with a chuckle. "Aren't you afraid of someone coming in and seeing you ride my hand like this? Better yet if your boyfriend wakes up, it's all over for you Jean."

Her words only caused the heat in my belly to further expand. *God I was so close.*

I looked down at her fully ready to glare but I couldn't. As soon as her hooded eyes met mine I could only lean forward and bring my mouth to hers. Her tongue invaded my mouth as if claiming me. It was messy, dirty, and *so wrong.*

"Tell me how much you like it," she whispered against my lips. "Tell me how much you get off on this. Get off on sneaking around behind his back. Get off on acting like this cute innocent little girl when really you're a fucking whore."

I couldn't. I really couldn't speak as my orgasm ripped through me for the second time. Tears sprang to my eyes and I choked out a sob against her.

She met my eyes with a devilish smirk.

"The next time I tell you to do something," she warned and gripped my chin, forcing me to look at her. "You do it or I'll have him walk in on me fucking you."

I swallowed thickly.

"You can't do this Shae, this was overboard," I said, shame filling my entire soul when I realized what just fucking happened.

"I can and I will. And you know what you will do?" she asked. "You are going to break up with him and get this tight ass of yours back to my place."

My eyes stung.

"No," I said with a shake in my words.

"Yes," she said harshly. "I'll give you by Friday. If you are not at my house that night you'll have bigger things to worry about than Hunter walking in on us." She stood up and dug in her pocket and threw a paper bag at me.

She walked to the door without another word. I looked inside the bag and my jaw dropped when I saw the amount of cash that was in there. This had to be enough money to cover a good amount of the debt. I didn't need to ask *how* she got this, only…

"Why?" I asked in a hollow voice.

She paused with her hand on the door. I could only barely see the expression on her face from my angle, but it hadn't been one that I saw often, and it stirred something inside me.

"I'm sorry about your mom," she said not looking at me. "She was a good woman."

She left me floundering for a response.

Jean

THREE YEARS EARLIER

I shifted uncomfortably under Shae's arm as we walked through the restaurant floor. The dim light made shadows crowd the patrons' faces and gave off an ominous feeling that hung in the air between us. Their leering gaze gave me goosebumps and made my already sweat-dampened skin feel even slimier. Smoke filled the air and crept into my lungs making my nose burn and my lungs feel heavy.

There was no way anything legal was happening in a place like this and I can't believe I let Shae talk me into this. It was beyond a bad idea, and I was woefully unprepared to schmooze the mafia.

The mafia for crying out loud!

Shae may have been excited to play these guys—and hell I was before as well—but now that I *actually* had to play a part, my anxiety shot through the roof. It was mid-winter and even though I was wearing a skimpy spaghetti strap dress, my skin was slick with sweat, and it was only getting worse as we walked further into the place.

"Lighten up, love," Shae whispered in my ear, her lips brushing across the sensitive flesh. "No one will dare harm you when you look so delicious."

Besides my buzzing mind, my skin began to heat in a different way.

I couldn't even protest if I wanted to because she quickly steered me towards a table that sat three people, one of which stood behind the other two acting as a guard. He eyed me suspiciously as we arrived.

"Shae, I didn't know your girlfriend was such a beauty," a man with a thick Russian accent spoke. He had dark hair and icy blue eyes that seemed to peer into my soul. He was wearing a black button-up that had the first few buttons undone and a glass of whiskey was already in his hand.

This man seemed like a dangerous one. It was in the way his eyes roamed the area slowly, there was no rush in his movements and even in an environment such as this, he was completely at ease.

"Surprised you stick with her," the other man spoke. He was soft-faced and had slicked-back black hair. His brown eyes raked over my form in ways that disgusted me. "She's lacking some serious equipment there." His eyebrows wiggled suggestively at me.

By the way Shae's arm tightened around my shoulder I could tell they were not friends.

"That's easily fixable with some silicone," I said with a sweet smile. "Not that we ever needed that before." I gave him a small smile. "I feel for the women who have partners that rely on only their short dick to please them."

There was an extended pause in which all of the ways that I could be killed entered my mind. Then the guy with the Russian accent let out a booming laugh that seemed to even cut through the loud noises of the restaurant.

"I like this one," he spoke. "She has balls."

Shae let out a chuckle.

"Jean, this is Anton." She waved to the Russian. "And this is Carlos."

Carlos' face was starting to flush but he nodded towards me

anyways. "They are good business partners that I have worked with for a long time."

"Four years next week," Anton said with a smile. "This is somewhat of a tradition for us."

I smiled at Shae as she pulled out my chair for me. A waitstaff came over almost immediately.

"I'll have a whiskey on the rocks," Shae said and looked towards me. "How you feeling tonight? Whiskey? Martini? Long Island?"

I smiled at her and looked towards the waitress. I would need to get really messed up to handle this night, my hands were already shaking so much that I had to ball them into fists and push them into my thighs to stop the shaking.

"A Long Island sounds delicious," I said.

She nodded and left our table.

My heart was pounding and the fear I felt only intensified as the men watched us. Even though my words came out flawless and the smile rested on my face, I was freaking out on the inside.

"Tell me you have some information about the Matisse," Carlos said then took a drag of a cigarette. "My contact has been nagging me about it for ages."

"Promising things we can't keep, Carlos?" Shae asked. There was a tone to her words I didn't like. It was accusatory, like they had been down this road one too many times. I looked between Anton and Carlos and then to the bodyguard behind them...my gut filled with lead. Immediately I began to understand that this was not the type of meeting that I wanted to be around.

"I'm going to the ladies' room," I whispered to Shae and moved to stand but her grip on my wrist stopped me. Her fingernails dug into my skin almost making me cry out. I stilled in my chair.

"Not at all," Carlos mumbled.

The waitress came back with our drinks, and I took a big gulp barely even pausing as the alcohol hit my tongue.

"Now that we have our drinks," Anton said and waved to the man behind him. "Let's get this thing going."

The guard nodded and moved to the edge of our table to face the rest of the room. I could hear a still crash through the room like a silent hurricane destroying everything in its path.

"Out," his voice was deep but barely above normal speaking tone.

Instantly the people in the room got up and left the area, not bothering to take their drinks. The mass movement of bodies was almost surreal to see, and I found myself rushing to catch up to what was happening. They all moved quickly, yet silently. Shae's grip on me was the only thing keeping me from running after them.

My smile dropped and I continued to sip on my drink, trying to prepare myself for this shit show. I shot Shae a look, but she was glaring daggers at Carlos and ignoring me completely.

When everyone had left the room Anton turned to Carlos and muttered simply, "Did you think you could get away with it?"

Carlos let out a huff and rolled his eyes.

"What are you talking about Anton?"

Shae took a sip of her own drink before answering.

"The guy you sold us out to was dirty before you even came into the picture," she said. "Really, nine grand and a shipment of cocaine was all that it took? Do you think we are stupid?"

Carlos' face placed considerably; his eyes darted to the guard that had cleared the room.

"What else did you tell them?" Anton asked with a raised brow.

"I didn't do what you guys think I did, okay?" he said quickly.

"Then what did you do?" Shae asked. "Cause it seems like you tried to sell us out because you didn't get what you wanted."

"It had nothing to do with you guys I swear—"

Anton moved in an instant and a gun was to Carlos' head. I saw a smile spread across Anton's face before a glass-shattering boom echoed through the room.

Don't throw up. Don't throw up. Don't throw up.

I squeezed my hand in Shae's and looked away from the dead body. I couldn't get the image of his brains exploding out of his skull out of my mind, nor the wheeze that came from his body after his head hit the table with a clunk.

"Drink," Shae said and forced me to look forward. "It will help."

Anton's eyes were staring into mine when I looked back up.

"Sorry my dear," he said. "Duty called, but don't worry. Shae has better loyalty than him. A good trait in a partner."

I grabbed my drink and in quick gulps finished it. They then had the audacity to continue talking as Carlos' dead body lay on the table. The blood seeped into the white tablecloth and slowly made its way towards Shae and me throughout the rest of our meeting.

I do not know how long it lasted, or how long I stayed staring at the blood seeping into the white cloth, but by the time Shae had told me it was time to leave I had felt like it was mere minutes.

That was the first night I left, and I didn't come back for weeks.

Shae

It wasn't hard to find out literally everything about Hunter and his parents. They seemed to love the media and the limelight so there were articles upon articles on them ranging from their latest advancements to his cousin, Misty, who had just won a medal for horseback riding back in Louisiana.

So right after Jean had run away from Alvaro's house I set my sights on the older couple we had seen at the gallery. A few calls later I had their names, and their son's name.

His father was easy to pull in. All I had to do was just ask Alvaro to drop a hint that I *might* be able to help out with some of their issues and—bam—I got invited to brunch.

Meeting Jean there was a nice surprise, though if I could gather anything from Hunter's texts, I knew that they would be there. I also found out a very interesting fact about Hunter that I was positive Jean didn't know.

It had been a while since I had to sneak around to get information on someone...but this was too good to miss. The last time I had done this was for a newly onboarded client after Jean had left me, so I was a bit rusty but excited to get in the game again.

When it happened last time, I was looking for anything to distract me from my rage and so I fell into a hole of constantly researching and investigating my own leads. It was a nice distraction but didn't last for long, and now I was here doing it *again* all for Jean.

Just like everything in my life revolved around that delicious vixen.

I followed Jean and Hunter to work that morning and watched as he dropped her off at work with a sloppy kiss on the lips. She tried to hide her grimace, but she failed miserably. I couldn't help the smug feeling that warmed my insides when I caught it. It was only a matter of time before she was at my doorstep once more...and I couldn't wait.

I was so lost in my daydream of seeing Jean in my bed once more that I almost missed him leaving. I started up my Toyota and tailed after him but made sure to stay far away enough that he didn't see me coming, not that he would know it was me anyways. This was the car I used for research and research only, so even if he had also done his research, he wouldn't even know what hit him when I spilled this all to Jean.

It wasn't long before I realized that this motherfucker wasn't going to work. Instead, he entered the parking lot of a fancy high-rise apartment building. I had an inkling where he was going. There were texts on his phone that spelled out, in detail I might add, what he was doing.

Instead of following him into the parking lot I circled around the back and parked my car behind a dumpster. I stepped out and rushed into the apartment with my hood up praying I didn't miss anything. I dressed for the occasion: a black hoodie, jeans, and a face mask.

When I entered the back I pushed through until the lobby elevator was in view. I cursed and ducked back behind a planter as the elevator door opened to reveal Hunter. He wore a button-up and slacks with his curly hair just barely combed out of his face. He didn't even glance towards the planter I was hidden behind and walked straight into the lobby where a group of normal-looking businessmen stood when they saw them.

There were three that I could count. I quickly pulled out my phone to snap a few pictures of them but froze when I zoomed in on the face of the man who was currently glaring daggers at Hunter.

Carter's phone call from Saturday morning rang through my head.

"William's boy?" Carter's gruff voice from the other end on the phone. I could hear the waves and honking of ships in the background. It was peak time for them to set out so while there was a chance he could be overheard, the noise even would cover any vital information he chose to spill.

"Tell me what he's up to," I said as I sat back in my office chair. "Anyone that uses you has to be in some dark shit."

I expected Carter to laugh but instead he let out a heavy sigh.

"I've been trying to raise the price on him," he said. "I want him and his dirty business out of here. I turn a blind eye to a lot of things but this... It's where I draw my line."

The seriousness of his tone made a shiver run down my spine. I had been doing business with him for years and not once have I heard him speak like this before.

"I want to help," I said.

He laughed at that.

"Lord I feel as though I am in trouble," he joked. "I'm not sure what else I can give ya Shae, but whatever you can do to get this guy out of my ports would be a godsend."

I let out a chuckle.

"Just your loyalty," I said and gave him a quick goodbye before dialing the next number. It picked up on the second ring.

"Special Agent Jonson," came a voice.

"Special agent," I purred. I heard a string of curses before hearing a shuffling.

"What do you want, Shae?" he asked in a whisper. I let out a laugh.

"Why are we whispering?" I said in a mocking tone. I nudged the mouse with my knuckle, my computer screen lighting up instan-

taneously showing a grainy picture of Hunter's shipments...and the people in them. "Afraid you'll get caught?"

"You're an informant... Your information needs to remain confidential," he said in an angry tone. I rolled my eyes. It's like he was saying it just in case someone was overhearing.

"I'm gonna send you someone," I said and hit send on the pre-typed email I had written up that included pictures.

"Who the fuck is this?" he grumbled on the other line losing all of his professional tone.

"Do your job and find out," I snapped at him. "There is a rat contaminating our ports and I expect that badge to actually work this time instead of lying on its ass and collecting government money."

I heard his angry breaths, but he didn't respond.

Good, he better not test me.

"Holy shit is this...?"

"Yes," I said with an overexaggerated tone. "When your wife finally sucks your dick after getting that promotion you will remember who to thank."

I wasn't here to collect information on them, but it couldn't hurt to take a picture and stash it away for later. Hunter looked visibly worried but continued to blab on as if he was talking to an old friend.

Figuring it wasn't going to get better than this, I snuck back to my car and drove to Hunter's work before he did. His father had invited me over today and I thought I would make good on that promise.

I wasn't surprised to see Hunter arriving an hour later and this time with his tall blonde secretary in his car. I knew who she was from their texts, but I didn't know how she got into her role or where she came from. Anton's guys were still looking into her after I reached out to them with almost zero leads. Anton had stayed with me the last few years and had proven to be valuable. I just hoped that he could find more information on her.

I steeled myself and pulled into a parking spot near Hunter's car. They had left only moments before I pulled up. I didn't care how casual I looked in the moment, I had no one to impress here and after this I would refuse to do business with them.

I had one thing to do today and then I would leave them forever.

Taking off my mask I entered the building and gave my name to the front desk lady. She smiled and called Mr. Williams to let him know that I had arrived. Instead of him coming down to get me he sent his assistant. I rolled my eyes his laziness.

When I did finally make it up into the office he started his whole lecture on how he had managed to build up such a company, even though I hadn't even asked. He was treating it like a personal tour.

The entire time I couldn't help but think that Hunter's father was just as spineless as he was. He was aging, poorly, and had only sustained business as long as he had because he exploited workers around the world to do his bidding.

I wondered just how much of Hunter's *real dealings* he knew about.

"Yes the whole team is in Malaysia," he said giving me a wink. "They are cheaper."

"I bet," I murmured and followed him around one of his many offices. The people there seemed to be just as miserable as I was, but some looked at me with curious glances. probably wondering what someone like me was doing here.

A smile spread across my face when I spotted Hunter in his office. The walls here were all made of glass, so I wasn't surprised to see him...or his secretary. They looked innocent from here, but I saw the way she twirled her hair and the way he leaned forward to get closer to her.

Even without reading his texts, what was happening between them was obvious.

"Ah there he is," Mr. Williams said and waved to Hunter. His eyes widened when he saw me next to his father and he paled considerably, no doubt remembering the day of the brunch. It flashed through my mind, and I couldn't help the sick satisfaction that rose in me.

I pushed him onto the couch, his eyes wide as he looked up at me.

"Stay quiet, pretend to be asleep and I'll give you a show," I ordered.

He sent me a glare.

"Did you put something in my drink?" he asked, speech still slurred.

"Just a very strong relaxant, but you won't be put to sleep," I said and walked over to the window, sitting down on the couch. "Lie down Hunter, I'm sure you'll be interested in seeing what happens with me and your girlfriend."

"What are you talking about?" he asked enraged.

"Does she know about your secretary?" I asked relaxing against the back of the couch. His pale expression told me all I needed to know. "I thought so. Now lie back and listen while I make your girlfriend come harder than you ever did. By the end of the week if you are not broken up I will single-handedly ruin your career."

He sputtered in anger, "You have nothing on me."

I rolled my eyes.

"Carter?" I asked innocently. "He may be a bitch and have no loyalty...but only to you."

"You bitch," he hissed at me.

"Yes now lie back and do as I say," I hissed. "You have no power here."

We heard the frenzied steps coming down the hall. If looks could kill I'd be dead twice over. He let out a groan and fell back on the couch with his eyes closed.

Not a moment later did Jean's face pop through the door.

Hunter left his office to come meet us outside. I sent him a smile playing the role of businesswoman even if I looked nothing like it.

"I'm here to talk about the exports," I said in a neutral tone. The redness started from under his collar and spread to his ears.

"Join me in my office," he said, and I followed him to the glass box with a wave to his father.

When I sat down in his office chair and he closed the door, he let out an angry breath. He had barely been able to hold in his angry expression though he sure as hell tried to.

"What are you doing here?" he asked.

I looked up at him from my seat in his chair giving him a bored expression.

"Just a check in," I said and picked the dirt under my nails. "Did Carter tell you he cannot work with you anymore?"

I could see him grinding his teeth together and if this was a cartoon, smoke would be billowing out of his ears.

"No," he spit out.

"Pity," I said in a sad voice. "Sorry to break the news to you but you have been officially kicked out. Your shipments will be rejected, and you will have to find another port."

"Is this really all because of Jean?" he asked, his hands balling into fists at his side. "Are you some obsessed freak or something?"

"It's because Carter works *for me*," I said in a low tone. "And I don't want to be tied to your shit."

He rolled his eyes.

"Whatever, I'll figure it out," he said. "You can leave now."

I shrugged, not bothering to tell him my special agent friend would reach out.

"Speaking of Jean," I trailed off looking at the gang of employees that watched us interact through the glass. They never left their seats, but their attention was zeroed in on us...even that secretary of his. "Did she dump your ass yet?"

"Wouldn't you know?" he asked with a scoff.

I cocked my head and looked at him with a bored expression.

"Obviously," I said. "So, you are supposed to reply with no and then I remind you that if she doesn't you must."

"You gave us until Friday," he reminded.

"And you watched your girlfriend come on my mouth," I said

with a smirk. "Twice. I would expect you to want to rid yourself of a girlfriend like that as fast as you could."

I watched him swallow and his hands turn into fists.

"You don't need to remind me," he hissed.

"You wanna know what else I've done to her?" I asked daringly.

I really shouldn't but the sooner he left her, the better. I wanted this fucker out of her life. I once thought that he was just a spiny little wimp that couldn't find the clit if you paid him, but looks are deceiving. He was dangerous and tried to play games with the big boys not knowing that they were going to fucking destroy him.

Just as she entered my mind the blond leggy secretary brought me a cup of hot coffee. I gave her a smile and took it from her.

"Tell me," I said to her. "Can he really not find the clit?"

She gasped loudly and looked at Hunter with an offended expression.

"Get out," Hunter commanded. When she left he took my coffee from my hands. "You don't need to be here, I get it. I'll end things with her."

"You better," I warned and stood. "And if I find out you stuck your filthy dick in her again I'll cut it off."

Hunter let out a deep chuckle.

"You're too late there," he said. "Just last night she rode me until she was shaking."

It was my turn to laugh.

"Yikes," I said. "That's sad for you."

I left him with no other explanation.

I WAITED FOR HER, like I promised. Though every day I did check Hunter's texts to see what he was up to. There was no indication that he was actually going to go through with it and the thought made my blood boil.

I played with the idea to hack into Jean's phone like I did Hunter's, but I knew it was crossing a line with her. I was okay fucking with Hunter's life but when Jean finally came back to me I wanted it to be on her own accord.

It was Wednesday morning when I got the call.

"I can't believe you," Jean hissed through the phone. "I knew you were fucking crazy, but I had thought that after three years you would have at least some decency. It was the only thing I had besides escorting—"

"Slow down," I commanded and looked at the time. It was barely seven-thirty. "What are you talking about?"

I had been up for nearly two hours by now, working on various admin tasks before the day began and just finished replying to emails. Irritation was prickling at my nerves. I didn't have enough coffee to deal with this just yet.

"What am I talking about?" She scoffed and I heard her angry footsteps in the distance. "You got me fired from my job!"

"I'm sorry to break it to you, love...but that wasn't me," I said and pulled up Hunter's texts on my desktop.

"How could it not be you?" she said in an angry tone. "You have literally been fucking with my life nonstop since we saw each other again. If you think this will get you your way you are mistaken. If anything, this just makes me hate you more."

Lies, I thought bitterly.

"You know you don't need a job if you come back," I reminded. "I can give you everything you need."

She let out a pitiful laugh.

"I'm not breaking up with him for you," she said. I gripped the counter harshly. I didn't want to be the one to break the news about Hunter to her. At this point I didn't know which was more twisted:

Having her figure it out on her own and come crying to me.

Or telling her just to watch her crumble.

I would have to leave telling her as a last resort.

"Jean," I said with a sigh. "You know you'll just end up here. Let me come pick you up."

"Stay away from me," she hissed. "You may act like you didn't do anything, but I fucking know it's you."

"Come here now or I tell your boyfriend about us," I threatened.

There was a pause as she weighed my words.

"Do it," she dared and hung up on me.

Well, there goes my leverage against her. Could Jonson work any fucking slower?

Jean

THREE YEARS EARLIER

How many times have I come back to her?

How many times have I left her?

I had lost count after a while, but it never changed anything, I knew that I would keep coming back to her until the day that I died.

It was toxic and so were we, but I couldn't imagine a life without Shae. Even if that meant that she would never love me.

Tonight, I was meeting her at a hotel bar that was not far from our home. She had told me last week that she was meeting yet *another* client and that she would like me to be there. Though that was before our big fight. I had no idea if she would still want me to come to this.

I had been held up at Caroline's for the past four days trying to convince myself not to come back and stay away for real this time, but it was hard. Caroline herself had told me to quit it and to just stay with her for the time being as her house was big enough for the both of us.

And it was, the money she got from running her escorting business was enough to get her a two-bedroom that could fit both of us comfortably without ever having to really talk to each other...but I didn't want to bother her.

I had done enough freeloading for a lifetime.

Not only was Shae literally paying for everything I ever needed, but Caroline had given me a job when I needed it the most and asking to crash at her place was just too much.

I don't know when I began to resent myself, but I felt it now more than ever. It was like a puddle of acid just sitting in my stomach, eating away at me. I wondered when it had gotten so bad. When did I start to hate myself so much?

When I entered the hotel I got my answer.

Shae was at the bar, her button-up stretched across her body as she leaned back into the counter with a drink in hand. She was in her element with a relaxed smile on her face and her eyes locked onto her client of the night.

This time it was a girl.

I felt a flash of bitterness as she trailed her hand up Shae's arm. The girl was pretty, model-like with blonde hair and blue eyes. Even from so far away I could see the shine of her white teeth in the dim light. I knew this was business, I had seen it... But the sour feelings that had been building in my stomach in that moment just seemed to explode.

But I am not her girlfriend, and she does not love me. The thought was so sudden and powerful that it seemed to pause even time.

Sure, Shae had said that I could be a sugar baby or even a girl-friend if I'd like...but she didn't *want* anything more. She never wanted to love anyone. Never wanted for anyone to stick around long enough to see her flaws. Girlfriend was just a pretty title to put on something that was hollow inside... It was all to placate me

It was obvious because every time I got too close, I was pushed away. Usually, it was what started our fights, then I would leave just like I did and when I came back I would tip toe around the very thing that started our fight.

But this wasn't what I wanted...*or was it?*

I wanted Shae... I knew that much...but like this? A Shae without a care for me like I cared for her?

I swallowed thickly when the girl leaned closer to Shae.

I took one hesitant step back, watching to see if Shae would even notice me here. The seconds went by and I could hear my heart beat with each second.

I turned back and left the hotel before I could change my mind. Shae didn't look at me, she was too wrapped up in her client of the night. I took this as a sign that we needed more time, that *I* needed more time.

It wasn't long before I found myself staring at our empty home. I fought to bring more of myself into this space, but it was still overshadowed by Shae and I could barely find myself in the room.

As I packed, my mind raced through the next steps.

I knew that I would be back at some point, but I couldn't reasonably give a date when and even though I felt calm and clear-headed now I knew that when I finally had a moment to think about my decision...I would be a mess.

Even now I felt my throat tighten and tears prick at my eyes.

This is for the best, I thought to myself. I paused at the room we shared, my hand brushing against the metal doorknob.

I wondered if she would hate me for staying away for so long. Another half of me wondered if she would try and come to find me when she realized that I wasn't coming back so easily now.

I had wished for the type of Shae that would hunt me down, confess her love to me, and steal me away like some twisted knight...but that was not her. She was more likely to sit and wait for me to come back because it was I who could not live without her, while she was perfectly fine without me.

When I was finally done I stood by the entrance staring at the same piece of artwork that had started it all. Back then I didn't know exactly what would happen between Shae and me...but I couldn't come to regret anything that I did.

I thought to leave her a note, maybe send her a text, or even call her. Letting her know that I was leaving but I would come back after I had some time to think... But when I moved to pull out my phone I found myself unable to complete the action.

Instead, I just shifted the bags that I had in my hand and with one last glimpse at the penthouse, I left for good.

Jean

I shouldn't have underestimated her.

I knew Shae was a fucked-up person that would do whatever she wanted to get her desired outcome...but I had foolishly thought that I was different. It was the same as last time.

Fool me twice, shame on me.

I rested my overfilled box on my hip as I took the elevator to my apartment. I hadn't realized how much stuff I had brought to the office until I was forced to pack it up as my coworkers stared at me.

It was humiliating and embarrassing but that wasn't even the worst part. No, what took the cake was that news of my escorting had been plastered on flyers and thrown around the office like confetti. My face burned when the patronizing stares of the ladies locked in on me and their whispers filled the offices.

I knew there was something weird about her.

No wonder she never talked to us. Didn't want us finding out.

What a whore.

Do you think the one that dropped her off was her client?

It was my worst nightmare all tied up into one disgustingly gaudy bow. I was fuming when I put together who could have done this but also incredibly ashamed. I knew this wasn't work that I would want others to know about, that's why I kept it hidden for so long. I wanted to tell them that I had no choice. That I had bills to pay and that without this job I would for sure be stuck out on the street with nothing to my name.

But instead, I just quietly followed my boss into his office and listened as he explained that I could no longer work there. While he was talking down to me I had a spark run through me and I almost wanted to fight him and tell him that firing me over this was unethical...but I kept my mouth shut and when he was done, I left without saying a word.

I shouldn't be relieved that I was finally out of that soul-sucking job, but a part of me deep down was completely and utterly ecstatic. While I had no idea what I would do about my debt, I could choose my path. I could brush off that old certificate and try my hand at something new.

Or at least that's what I had disillusioned myself to believe until my phone vibrated in the box with my father's number lighting the screen.

God damn it.

I took a deep, calming breath before answering.

"I paid the late fees," I said without a greeting.

"I know," he trailed. His voice sent a pang through my chest. I missed him. A lot.

I had grown up having a good relationship with him, and was completely blindsided when he left us. I couldn't believe that the man who had kissed my bruises and protected me from monsters was so twisted and evil inside that he would leave his dying wife.

"Then what do you want?" I asked as I pushed the door to my apartment open. I halfway threw my box onto the counter in my anger.

"I was worried," he said. "And I wanted to reach out because..."

He was trying my patience.

"Spit it out."

"Where did you get so much money?" he rushed out.

I let out a bitter laugh. Apparently everyone cared so much about what I did on the side now.

"None of your business," I spat. "Don't go acting like a father now. That ship has sailed."

He cleared his throat then sighed.

"I watched you grow up, Jeanie," he said. "I still care for you even if our relationship has been rocky the last few years."

My eyes stung at the use of my childhood nickname.

"Rocky?" I asked my voice cracking. "You left us when mom was *dying.* It's not rocky, it's destroyed. How could you fucking do that to us?"

"Jean."

"And leave me with the bill?"

"I tried to offer—"

"Don't bullshit me, Jim," I said. "Don't call me again and don't act like you care about what I do to pay back the fees. Just go on back to your sweet little life with that bimbo wife of yours and your stupid fucking kids."

I hung up before he could say anything and before he could make me feel bad about my words.

I let out a scream that had been bubbling in my throat and brought down my fist onto the counter. The pain helped center me for the moment, allowing me to take a breath of air.

I longed to call Shae again. She would take my mind off of it and know exactly what to say. All I could think about was how wonderful it would be to curl up in her arms and forget I even existed.

Instead I picked my phone up to call Hunter.

"Babe?" he asked after the second ring. "Are you okay?"

The words seemed to curl up and die in my throat before I could even form a coherent thought.

How would I even begin to tell him what happened with my work? And why it happened?

A small part of my brain told me I shouldn't do this, that he was not the person that I should be relying on in this situation... But I ignored it.

"I...had a fight with my dad and left work early," I said after a moment of floundering for an excuse.

I could hear the creak of his office chair between our silence.

"Well uh..." He paused. "I'm sorry baby. How about this... Let me skip the rest of the day and come home to binge some shows and pig out with you? We can forget this day ever happened."

My whole body felt tight.

"Sure baby," I said. "Sounds great."

"I'll see you in thirty!"

The call went dead.

I sighed and placed my phone down on the counter.

Fuck.

~

I SCRAMBLED to find a place to hide my box of shit before settling on a remote part of the closet and dressing in my pajamas. I opened a bottle of wine before Hunter got home for looks, but also to drown myself before my guilt did first.

I drank the first half-empty bottle in under ten minutes and was on to my next one just as Hunter showed himself in the door-way. He was dressed in his button-up and slacks and his hair was slightly disheveled, no doubt from trying to clear up at work before coming home to me.

He is too good of a boyfriend to me.

"Aw, you got started without me?" he asked and wiggled his brows at me. When he closed the door I noticed that he had his hands full with white plastics bags. The worn logo on the side told me they were from the corner store.

"Long day," I said with a sheepish smile. "Whatcha got there?"

He gave me a grin and hoisted the bags up onto the counter before pulling out not one but three tubs of ice cream.

"I have rocky road for me, pistachio for you, and double brownie fudge for when you get so drunk you forget chocolate makes your stomach hurt," he answered with a slight teasing tone.

The stone in my stomach seemed to grow twice in size at his admission.

"Let's do it," I said and turned on the T.V. to rewatch *Teen Mom* for the tenth time.

"Oh this is my shit," Hunter said with a laugh. "Let me go change before we get into it."

He reappeared only moments later in sweatpants and no shirt. Even though I felt horrible and my emotions were all in knots, I had to admit that he does have a nice body. His chest is smooth and slightly defined. He doesn't have abs but his torso is lean and there is a small trail of hair under his belly button that leads south.

"Give me that look and we won't even get through episode two," he playfully threatened.

I let out a small laugh and curled closer to Hunter as he sat on the couch. He reached over the back to grab out blankets and prop them over us. I sighed and sunk into him. *This is nice.*

Hunter was right though. We didn't even make it through the full first episode before he had taken the wine glass out of my hands and began trailing kisses down my neck.

"Now I *really* know why you came home," I teased but wrapped my arms around his shoulders pulling him closer to me.

"You got me," he said in a husky voice against my neck. I tried to pull him up to plant a kiss on his lips but instead he pushed me back into the couch and tugged my shirt over my head.

I didn't let the thoughts of how fucked this was enter my head, instead I just helped take off my bra and moan as his tongue circled my nipple.

"Hunter," I said in a breathy voice. A pang shot through me as he bit down onto my nipple.

"You know if you worked with me we could sneak into the supply closet." He continued to kiss south as he spoke against my skin. He ripped my shorts off in one motion. I gasped and tried to cover myself but he smacked my hands away. "Take an empty meeting room." He kissed my mound, his hazel eyes narrowing at me. "Everyone would know what we were doing. I'd want them to."

My throat tightened. This was not normal. This was not Hunter. He had never gone down on me before and never been so rough. I liked rough, always have. A little bit of pain went a long way when mixed with pleasure but this was not that.

"Hunter you don't have to—"

I was cut off when he brought his mouth down to my clit and sucked hard.

"I want to babe," he said. "I am feeling particularly ravenous today."

∼

I DIDN'T COME EVEN though Hunter had managed to—*finally* —find the clit.

Instead I faked it the best I could and he came up with a mischievous grin. I didn't dare break his heart and tell him that I didn't come even as he surprised me by pulling me into a hug and cuddling me on the couch.

"I mean it babe," he whispered in my ear. His fingers came to rub patterns up my arm. "Come work with me at my dad's. It will be better pay than whatever your job is paying you now."

He planted a kiss on the spot behind my ear.

"I'll think about it babe," I whispered.

I could feel his sigh behind me.

"Anyways, there is a client dinner that I need to get to tonight, would you mind being my hot date?" he asked in a slightly suggestive tone.

I turned to raise my brow at him.

"You want *me* to come to a client meal?" I asked disbelievingly. This was an escort job, not a girlfriend's job. I had no social standing and would just be treated as eye candy.

"Could be *your client* if you come to work for me," he said.

"So now it's for you?" I asked irritation filling me. He rolled his eyes at me.

"You know that's not what I mean," he said with a huff. "Please babe?"

I swallowed my words and sat. After a moment I put on my underwear and walked towards the bedroom.

"Sure babe, I will take a bath to get ready," I said and ducked into the room without waiting for his response.

MORE THAN A FEW hours later I was stuck in the back of an Uber in the dress I *just so happened* to forget to return to Caroline. Hunter was at my side typing furiously on his phone and I was trying to look out the window and calm my racing heart.

Just treat it like another job, I told myself. *Get in. Laugh at their jokes. Then leave.*

We pulled up to a building that was unknown to me and walked silently into the lobby. There was a person there to direct us but it seemed like Hunter already knew where to go and walked past her without even a glance.

He brought us to the elevator in the back of the lobby and pressed the button for the fifth floor. There was light music that played in the background, breaking our silence and the tension that grew between us.

"The client is the one my father's contact, Shae, introduced me to," he said and I tried not to freeze at *her* name. "Jonson, and he insists on having dinner with her there so we have to suffer through her games yet again."

I swallowed thickly, sweat coating the back of my neck.

"Games?" My voice came out in a squeak.

Hunter gave me a look and opened his mouth to speak but the elevator dinged open. He looked from the floor beyond and back to me before shaking his head and grabbing my elbow, dragging me along with him.

The whole floor was dim and the dark walls seemed to only make it all the more sinister-feeling. The floor was a dark red and there were round tables in the middle of the room, almost all of them filled with men in suits. They were drinking, laughing, and even smoking. The worst part was there was not a woman among them and they all turned to stare at me as I walked with Hunter.

Luckily we were headed to the back where there seemed to be more private dining areas. While there were still no closed doors, they had coverings on the top and waist-high barriers around each table, and where the little nooks connected there were walls. So while I could see the people at the table as I walked towards them, we would not be able to see the people on either side of us.

This is dangerous, my senses told me.

I had been in a place like this. One that smelled of crumpled used bills, smoke, and something metallic. This is where underground business was done, not where a good, god-fearing boy should be.

I shot Hunter a glance but he was too occupied with the table we were headed to. His gaze darkened as we got closer, as if he already hated this Jonson guy.

I looked towards the table and saw, as he promised, Shae sitting there in a button-down shirt and slacks. Even though I had seen her not that long ago, being here with her now felt like coming home after a long time.

...and it scared me.

I wanted to run to her. Bury myself in her arms and lose myself in her scent. I didn't want these problems, or this life... I felt like I was at my breaking point.

I almost forgot about Hunter until his finger gripped into my skin. That's when I noticed the other man, Jonson. He was younger than I thought and much taller as well. He had to be over six feet tall—he looked cramped in the nook as he stood.

His black hair was slicked back and he had a small mustache that was neatly trimmed. His grey eyes shifted between Hunter and me, but instead of looking over my form in a disgusting fashion as I expect a man like him to do, his eyes focused on where Hunter held me at my elbow.

It was enough to stir me out of my stupor.

"You must be...Jonson, is it?" I asked him with a smile and used my free arm to reach out to him. He smiled and covered his hand in mine. It engulfed my own.

"You can call me Nick," he said with a smile. "Please sit, drinks will be here soon."

The choice was either to sit by Jonson or to sit by Shae. Hunter seemed to notice this and paused before sitting me next to Shae. Her eyes did not meet mine as I sat and instead focused on a particular spot on the table. When I sat down Hunter's hand formed a vice grip on my upper thigh, all while meeting Jonson's eyes.

They quickly jumped into small talk, beginning to bond on football of all things. I didn't understand it, nor could I follow what they were on about. I tried my best to not look at Shae and focused on Hunter and Jonson.

They were interrupted by a waiter bringing in the drinks. Four glasses of whiskey. Hunter gave me a look before turning to the waiter.

"Do you have wine for the lady?" he asked in a pleasant tone. I could feel the heat starting its attack from my neck all the way up to the tips of my ears.

"She's a big girl," Shae said breaking her silence. I forced my eyes down to Hunter's hand on my thigh. It was tightening. "She can take some whiskey."

I reached for the glass, only for my hand to be pulled back by Hunter.

"Wine, please," he said to the waiter once more.

The waited nodded and practically ran out of the room.

"More for me," Jonson said in a smooth tone and reached over to grab my whiskey with a wink. "Shae, why don't you take the lady to the balcony for some fresh air?"

"She's good here," Hunter practically growled.

Jonson looked slightly put off by his hostile tone.

"I would like to discuss the contents of the shipments and I am sure we don't need to bore her with these details. Unless..."

Hunter's jaw flexed and he reluctantly let go of me. He sent me a tense smile.

"I'll be done soon, babe. Be good and we can leave soon."

I nodded and got up on shaking legs. I was not made for this world. I knew it from the start with Shae. But how the fuck did Hunter get involved? Was this Shae's fault as well?

Shae's hand on my elbow was a grounding force and was everything I needed to continue back out into the room of leering men and to a well-hidden entrance to a balcony. Hunter and Jonson thankfully, would not be able to see us here.

"What the fuck is this, Shae?" I hissed as soon as the door shut behind us. The cold air whipped against my face like a slap and I suddenly regretted not bringing a coat.

"Business," she answered in a clipped tone. "Now you want to tell me why hell Hunter brought you here? And why you somehow think your job fired you? Oh ya and the biggest..." She stepped closer to me, invading my space and stared down at me with a nasty glare. "Why the fuck are you still with him?"

I was at a loss for words. She was too close, her scent and heat filling up the space around us. Suddenly I was shivering for a different reason.

"He asked me," I said in a weak voice. "If this is his business why are you here?"

"You missed two questions," she said with a growl.

"A truth for a truth," I bargained.

At that her eyes flashed with something for a moment before

she stepped back. I only then noticed how high we were, and how just behind the balcony was a five-story drop.

At least with Shae in front of it...it didn't bother me as much as it used to.

"I want to make sure this is done," she answered. "I do not want him near my ports."

I rolled my eyes at her.

"Your jealousy is not cute," I commented and crossed my arms over my chest.

"Believe it or not," she said with a frown. "Not everything in my life revolves around you. Your turn."

"You should know about the job part though," I said and glared at her. "Who else would print out flyers about my escorting and throw them all over the office."

She raised a brow at this.

"Please, I am classier than that," she said. "If I *really* wanted you to quit your job I would have found a way."

"There is no one else who would benefit from it," I hissed at her. "Now your turn, the truth. Why did you force me out of my job?"

She let out a sigh and ran her hand through her hair. I noticed she left the rings at home today.

"I didn't, Jean," she said. "I promise."

I held my breath for a moment before nodding and looking towards the floor. *I am still not fully convinced.*

"I..." I couldn't get the thought out. As soon as the words hit my tongue they felt weird and caused my mouth to dry.

"Are you really that in love with him that you want to stay?" she asked, her voice becoming softer than I had heard it in years.

I met her gaze and felt my heart stop. Her eyebrows were pushed together and her brown eyes looked like they were begging me to say anything other than...

"Yes," I whispered, my voice almost carried away by the wind. "I want to make it work."

"But that's not love," she insisted taking another step forward.

I took a step back this time, keeping the space between us. The closer she got the harder this would be.

"It was never love with us either," I said. "You made that very clear."

The door opened to save me a response from Shae. Nick's smiling face showed itself and he stepped onto the balcony with us.

"Talk is done," he said. "Pleasure doing business with you." He turned to me and gave me a sad smile while putting his hands in his pocket. "If you ever need help—"

"It's not like that," Shae's tone was curt as she cut him off. "She works with me. My assistant. No help needed."

I opened my mouth to yell at her but was interrupted by Nick's laugh.

"Is that how you do it, you little shit?" He laughed then shook his head.

"Yes and if you want to keep our relationship I suggest you get the fuck out of here before he thinks anything of it," she warned. Her eyes told me I better keep my mouth shut.

He rolled his eyes and waved to her as he left the balcony.

"Shae—"

"Tomorrow, seven o'clock," she said, her eyes still trained on the door. "I suggest you don't tell your boyfriend."

"I already—"

"Ten grand," she interrupted. "Just for the day. Give me one day. No funny shit."

I swallowed the lump in my throat.

"Twenty," I countered.

Her eyes lit up at that.

"Under your mat in the morning," she said. "So that you know I won't go back on my word."

Shit.

I wanted to respond but Hunter was the next person out onto the balcony. Suddenly the fear of falling off this balcony hit me like a tidal wave.

"Let's go," he barked.

I left Shae's side without looking back.

As I lay next to Hunter that night, I couldn't help but see Shae's face behind my closed eyes. There were so many questions that I had, yet to be answered.

Why was Hunter involved in this stuff?

Why did she continuously try to ruin my relationship?

What was her motive for coming back after all these years?

Those were the ones that stayed at the forefront of my mind but there were deeper ones, more dangerous ones swimming below the surface just waiting for their chance to strike.

Does she love me? Is that why she wants me back?

Is she thinking about me right now?

Had she waited?

What if I took her up on her offer tomorrow?

What if I left Hunter for her?

Do I still love her?

Could I forgive her?

The more I stared at the black ceiling the more the deepest thoughts seemed to take over. My body felt like it was almost vibrating with anticipation of tomorrow.

I honestly didn't care about the money anymore. Debt be dammed. All I could think about was what this meant for me.

For us.

The most terrifying thing was that *us* stopped meaning Hunter and myself, it now meant Shae and me.

And it felt right.

With a newfound resolve, finally I was able to drift into sleep excited for the next day.

THERE WAS a switch that happened in me last night as I was staring at the dark ceiling.

Hunter was next to me lying in the bed, his back towards me and loud snores tumbling out of his mouth. As soon as we had got home there was barely a sentence spoken between us and it remained that way until we went to bed.

Everything about Hunter seemed different since the day he came home and I couldn't get the way he looked at me and Shae out of my mind.

What did he know?

Could he sense something was happening?

In that moment in the darkness I had come to almost an acceptance of what was happening. I could never get away from Shae, I had tried so many times and I still ended up coming right back to her. I found my mind trailing towards her even as Hunter dragged me from the restaurant, even as he slept next to me, even as he brought me flowers, and took me out. There was never a time where she was far from me.

And I felt safe in that fact.

I was content to always be so wound in her because I couldn't think of a life without her even to this day.

For years I had tried to run away from her, but she was always there in the shadows following me as I did my day-to-day. Even my own mother had asked about her on her *death bed* for god's sake.

The night left and I found myself drifting in and out of a restless sleep with Shae's eyes constantly following.

I snuck out of the bed when the first rays of sun hit our room. Hunter had yet to stir and I really didn't know how I could look him in the eyes after last night.

I had made my decision and it wasn't one that I was proud of but it was one that I knew I couldn't run away from anymore. I had *tried* to be a good girlfriend. I had tried to change my life and forget her once and for all, but it was all too painful now.

Not ten minutes later I was entering a coffee shop with my

head still foggy from the lack of sleep. I had a plan—*a good one*—and for it I needed to be awake and prepared for anything.

Today would mark the first day where I would stop lying to myself.

"Jean?" a familiar voice called from the front of the shop.

I had just ordered and was waiting for the coffees near the end of the bar. Nick, the person who was working with Shae and apparently Hunter, was walking towards me with a smile on his face.

His enthusiasm made my head hurt.

I forced a small smile on my face.

"You're up early," I noted. "And coincidentally at the *same* coffee shop as me."

He let out a laugh and ran a hand through his hair.

"I come here all the time," he said. "And had to get *something* to keep me going after last night."

I nodded and watched as the baristas handed out drink after drink.

"Why did you ask me if I needed help last night?" I asked.

He paused and shifted on his feet so his face was hidden from me. When he looked at me again his face was relaxed.

"I just thought Hunter was a bit angry in there and it worried me," he answered. "Wanted to make sure that you were safe, even if it is just for work."

I felt the heat rise up my neck and to my face.

"I am fine," I said quickly and looked down at my feet.

"I still can't believe Shae made you get close to that bastard," he grumbled.

An uneasy feeling settled over me.

What did he know about Hunter that I didn't?

Everyone here seemed to be involved in something bigger than this but it was only I that was left out this entire time. I vowed to myself that I would try and get something out of Shae before the day ended.

Just then the barista called my name. I gave an apologetic

smile to Nick and went to leave but his hand caught my elbow. His eyes burrowed into mine before he spoke.

"Really though, if you need anything you can trust me," he said and put a card in my hand.

When I finally was able to push myself out of the cafe I threw his card into the trash without a moment of hesitation.

Shae

I let out a breathless sigh as I finally moved the last piece of furniture in place in my office.

Before it was just a large desk, a few monitors, and a bookshelf. I didn't allow people in here before so I never had the need to actually furnish it...but now I had an excuse.

And I had to make it happen in under twelve hours.

I had moved some of the furniture from the guest room and placed it in here to make it more comfy. A small couch was now pushed against the wall facing the wall of windows to my left. I moved some of the fake plants from the various rooms and put them in corners of the room to brighten up the space. I also stole the desk chair from the master to put on the other side of my desk so that I could sit with Jean while I worked.

I was somewhat...excited to finally have her back in the house again. It had taken so long to get to this point and *finally* she would be here in only a few minutes.

It was a win in my book...except for the confession she told me last night.

That made my chest ache.

But there was also a sliver of hope because she didn't say she

149

was in love with him, she said she wanted to make it work and today I would help her realize it wouldn't work.

But before that...

The doorbell rang.

I straightened my hair and smoothed down my wrinkled t-shirt. With a deep breath I walked from the office to the front door. When I opened it I was treated with a sight that made me smile.

Jean.

In a hoodie and jeans with two cups of coffee in her hands. Her hair was tied up into a messy bun and she didn't have an ounce of makeup on.

I loved it, every last bit of it down to her mismatched socks.

"You are casual today," she noted and walked in without taking off her shoes. "I thought I'd dress like this to annoy you but it looks like you beat me to it."

I smiled at her and took the hot coffee out of her hand. She sipped on the iced one with a look in her eyes that made my heart skip a beat.

God I'm acting like a god damn puppy. And all because I finally got her into my house again.

"Look at you," I teased. "Already such a good assistant."

I tried to hold in the grimace when the overly sweet coffee exploded on my tongue.

"You know me," she said with a smile. "Had to go get my boss her favorite caramel macchiato with four additional pumps and extra caramel drizzle."

I swallowed down the liquid sugar and placed my hand on her head, patting it softly.

"You did good," I said. "Let's get to work."

I led her back into the office and to my desk. I let her keep her shoes on even though the invisible dirt tracking severely irritated me. I pulled out a MacBook from my desk drawer and handed it to her.

"Oh, so you like *actually* want me to help you?" she asked, the shock evident on her face.

"Ya," I said. "I *actually* need help."

"Shae—"

I cut her off with a wave.

"None of the dangerous shit," I said. "Let's start with emails for my legit businesses then, if you want, later you can get on the fun stuff."

She accepted the computer hesitantly, moving her iced coffee out of the way. She reached over to the end of the desk and placed it on a coaster without me even having to ask.

God I wanted to take her right now.

But I would wait for the right time.

"Nick is not a ports guy, is he?" she asked as she opened the laptop. I tried not to bristle at her quickness. "Password?"

"The day I met you," I said and sat down in my chair. I had positioned my monitors so that I would have a clear view of her and I basked in the way her cheeks flamed.

"I don't remember the exact day," she said softly.

"September third," I replied and watched her as I sipped my coffee.

"Jonson?" she reminded.

"I can't tell you if you are still with that dumbass," I said. "That part of my business is confidential until you two break up."

It wasn't, but I didn't know what else to say to keep it from her and to keep her here.

"The fun stuff," she said in a dull voice.

I let her mess around with the computer for a bit, watching her closely.

It had been years since I was able to do this and even though I wanted her so bad I ached... I found myself able to wait. Maybe it's because I counted this as a win. Here she was with me, for the entire day.

"So are you really just going to stare at me while I do this?"

she asked. "And really just reply to emails? What changed from Labor Day until now?"

I let the smirk play at my lips.

"Are you asking why I am not trying to bend you over the table and fuck your brains out?" I asked. "Is that something you need from me, love?"

The fire in her eyes only stroked my inner fire.

"I don't *need* anything from you," she hissed.

"Tell me," I said with a hum. "Your boyfriend doesn't know you are fired right?"

She nodded slowly.

"And he doesn't know about your debt?"

She shifted in her chair.

"Not the amount," she whispered. Her plump lips turned into the cutest pout.

"Or the due date I'm guessing," I mused. "And definitely not the escorting."

She glared at me.

"The point," she demanded.

"It seems like I am the only one here who knows the whole story," I said. "And here you are sitting so patiently in my office, playing assistant for someone you said you hate."

She had no response.

"Seems like you need a lot from me," I said and leaned forward. She froze. "Secrecy, money, reassurance, and I guess we can add a couple of orgasms on there too since he is so incapable."

I was afraid I crossed the line there for a moment but she took a steadying breath and zeroed in on the laptop in front of her.

I watched her for another moment before turning to my own laptop. I fell into my normal working rhythm. On this desktop I had access to everything I needed but hers was a clean version. I may want her back in my life but I was only willing to show her so much. That was until I was sure about her.

She let out a heavy sigh only thirty minutes into the work.

"Why are you so different?" she asked.

Without looking at her I responded, "I'm not different."

"I thought we were past lying to each other," she said with a sweet tone. "You watched me leave for three years and all of a sudden you want me to come back and be a fucking assistant? Don't kid me."

I rolled my eyes and gave her a hard stare. She fidgeted in her seat, her eyes trained onto her lap.

"No, I want to fuck your brains out senseless and bind you to the fucking table until the thought of leaving tears your soul out," I hissed. I didn't mean for it to come out so snappy.

"Why three years later?" she pushed.

I let out a growl and pushed my chair back so I could lean over the desk and bring my face as close to hers as possible. Those stupid doe eyes widened in surprise.

"I gave you time," I said.

"But you only spurred into action when you saw me with Gary," she said, not backing down. Her body straightened and her wide eyes narrowed. "If you didn't see me at that party would you have still come for me?"

"No," I admitted. She recoiled as if slapped.

"Why?" she whispered.

"Because it was a promise I made myself," I said. A wave of uneasiness washed over me. I didn't want to talk about this yet. "I wouldn't seek you out, I wouldn't text, wouldn't call. You either came to me or if it was fate then we would meet."

She raised a brow at me.

"Since when do you believe in faith?" she asked.

"It's just a way to keep boundaries," I said with a grumble and stood back up.

"You, boundaries?" She laughed at this. "Where did you learn that? Therapy?"

I glared at her.

"You could have come back too," I noted. "Why didn't you?"

She looked back down at her hands.

"My mom got sick," she admitted. "I was taking care of her up until her death last year."

My heart pumped in my chest and roared in my ears.

"Are you saying you would have come back?" I asked.

She looked up with a pained expression.

"I loved you," she said. "Of course I would have."

Fuck waiting.

I shot forward and yanked her up by her shirt collar, forcibly bringing her lips to mine. She gasped at my actions and I could hear the coffee fall onto the desk and spill but I couldn't find myself to care about it. The taste of the coffee on her lips and her tongue exploring my mouth was a far better distraction.

The fire between us was roaring after so long of not being satiated. Every touch, every movement was making me lose my grip on reality.

I pulled her further and this time she surprised me by climbing onto the table. As our lips disconnected she used this chance to take off her hoodie. My mouth dried when I saw she wasn't wearing a bra underneath.

What a little liar.

She was at the perfect height for me to lean down just slightly and bring her erect nipple into my mouth. She let out a strangled moan and wrapped her hands through my hair. I gripped her hips to keep her in place as I assaulted her nipples, sucking them and biting them until she was writhing. I loved the noises coming out of her mouth. They were sweet and needier than ever.

"Lie back," I growled at her.

She looked down at the monitors around us, hesitating. Without wasting a moment I pushed everything to the ground and pulled her legs around for her. With a yelp she fell back onto the desk.

"Shae, your stuff," she protested as I slipped her shoes off.

"You don't care about that shit," I said and quickly unbuttoned her pants. "I should have known you couldn't resist. You were just waiting for me to break weren't you?" I scoffed and lowered to place a kiss right under her navel. "Such a fucking liar."

She was the one to start pushing down her pants. Her enthusiasm only fanned the flames roaring inside me and I pulled them the rest of the way off. She was left in lacy black underwear but with one look I could see her juices coating her inner thighs.

"You were really just sitting there all worked up weren't you?" I asked with a laugh. "What was it that turned you on, huh?"

I lowered myself in between her legs and left kisses up her right thigh. They flexed around my head and her fingers pushed me closer to her wet underwear but instead of complying like my body wanted me to, I bit the inside of her thigh.

"Tell me you want this," I demanded and licked the spot I just bit. She rewarded me with a moan. She was breathing deeply now, her body arching then sinking against the table with each gulp.

"I want this," she whined and pushed my head again.

Music to my fucking ears. I was about to come on the spot.

"Why?" I pushed, biting her other thigh before licking it. She moaned at this.

"I've never stopped wanting you," she said.

I rewarded her by running my tongue up the length of her underwear. A sweet tanginess exploded on my tongue and I hummed against her.

"I need more," I said against her. I felt her whole body shudder. "Why now?"

"I just want a release," she said and spread her legs further, enticing me. "You're right about one thing—Hunter cannot make me come."

A bitterness so strong shot through me that I almost wanted to push her off this table and demand she leave right this instant. But instead I stood up and reached for my belt. She watched me with heated eyes as I did so.

She looked beautiful splayed all over my desk. Her bun had come undone and her hair spread across the table and off the edge. She was barely holding onto the desk, her head was almost hanging off it.

"Turn around," I commanded and pulled the belt fully off.

She swallowed, her eyes trailing my form then like I asked, turned over on the desk so her ass was now pushed against me.

"Hands," I snapped. Her hands came behind her back almost immediately and she waited patiently for me to move.

At least she still remembered.

I wrapped the belt tightly enough around her wrists that they would constrict her movements but not blood flow. I'm sure by the end of this they would be bruised and she would have to go back to that *piece of shit* with evidence of what we had done.

I reached into the desk drawer and pulled out the strap-on that I kept hidden there. It was bigger than the ones we used to frequently use before and bright green, but it would have to work.

I pushed my pants off my hips and expertly fastened the straps. With each movement she squirmed in front of me.

"You're in luck," I said in a dark voice filled with venom. "I knew you would cave."

She didn't answer. I gritted my teeth together and pulled down her underwear, exposing her slick pussy in all its glory.

"I would have let you work like a little assistant and earn your keep without forcing this on you," I said and kneeled between her now spread legs.

I attacked her folds like a starving woman. She bucked and screamed against me but I used my hands to keep her legs and cheeks spread. I circled her hole before descending onto her clit and sucked as hard as I could. She froze against me before the cries started.

"Who's the liar now?" she asked through her sobs. "We both knew you just wanted me here to fuck me, nothing else."

I growled against her rose. She pushed her ass back into me, pushing against the bright green dildo. I teased her entrance with it, even though I knew she wasn't fully ready for it yet. If I was feeling a bit less bitter I may have hung on despite her pleas... But inside I wanted it to hurt.

I pushed into her with one thrust with my hand wrapping around her wrists, pulled her back into me.

She let out a cry and arched off the table.

"I would have let you live your days here, working for me until you were finally ready, but now I know it is you who had other things in mind," I growled and pulled out fully before snapping my hips into her once more. She let out a loud moan that reverberated off the walls. "You want to be treated like a common piece of meat?"

She let out a strangled noise as I began pounding into her at a frenzied pace.

"Oh my god," she moaned.

"Admit it," I demanded. "Stop lying to yourself."

"Not common," she said with a whine. "Just yours. Only yours."

"Fuck," I groaned and wrapped my hand through her wavy hair. I lifted her head so she was arched uncomfortably on the table. I wanted her to know who was in charge. That even though she was asking for this, I would take it my way and my way only. "You're saying you want me to pay you to be my whore?"

"Every day," she admitted.

I reached down and pinched her clit with my free hand, it was enough to make her scream and freeze, her orgasm tearing through her so violently that her scream stopped completely.

"Twenty grand is not just one fuck," I whispered and left a kiss on her back before biting down.

"As much as you want, all day," she promised, her voice ragged.

"Everyday," I reminded and moved against her.

The thought of having her here every day was almost enough to completely wash away my bitterness, but it lingered in the recesses of my mind... taunting me. Reminding me that she didn't want anything I was offering and instead played me at my own game.

We will see about that.

"Please again," she begged against me and pushed back into the strap.

Jesus Christ, she is going to ruin me.

"Fuck yourself," I demanded. And removed my hands from her completely.

She spurred into action, trying her best to fuck herself on the dick but with her hands tied behind her back and her position bent over the table she could only manage small thrusts back.

"Please Shae," she whimpered. "Just fuck me."

"I have to pay and do the work?" I teased. "It seems like I'm the one losing here."

She stood up straight against me. It took all my strength to not pull her against me and fuck her. I stepped back and sat down back onto my chair. She climbed over my lap with a determined expression and sunk down onto the cock. She threw her head back, baring her throat to me as she positioned herself.

I swallowed thickly and took in every detail hungrily. She was just as beautiful as I remembered. Breathtaking actually. I now have no idea how I lasted these last few years without her. It was like the world was dull and grey before and now it was vibrant and I was absolutely consumed by the goddess in front of me. With each swivel of her hips I felt like more of the world came back to me.

This was how it was supposed to be.

We were always meant to end up here together, I was sure of it.

I believed so deeply in my soul that she was who was meant to be in my life.

It was her that controlled me so fully. And I found myself no longer caring.

I straightened and cupped the back of her neck, bringing her lips down to mine. I gave her a passionate kiss, relearning all the crevices of her mouth and getting lost in her sweet taste. When I finally pulled away I sucked her bottom lip into my mouth and bit it lightly. Her hooded eyes followed my actions.

This is it, my mind chanted. *Say it. Say it. Say it.*

"Jean, I—"

"Don't think this means I forgive you," she said cutting me off. "This changes nothing between us. I still hate you."

How could one's heart explode so violently and their chest still be intact? Because mine felt like it was no longer in my chest. Even as I stared at her and gripped her hips as she rode to her climax... I couldn't bring myself back together.

The world that was so bright and beautiful was now too painfully clear.

I rubbed circles into her clit and watched as she shuddered on top of me. When she had finally come down off her orgasm I gave her a tight smile.

"Go wash up and get redressed," I said. "I have a brunch meeting and you are welcome to come."

She nodded and got off me. A loud squelching filled the room.

God I was fucked.

Jean

I didn't anticipate actually having to work for Shae.

In our last life together I was adamant to not be involved after I saw the murder of someone right in front of us. It wasn't the killing that scared me, I got over that trauma in time...but it was the way Shae reacted.

She acted as if though this was a normal occurrence and continued on with her conversation as if a dead body was not slumped over the table in front of us.

It was the start of the downfall of our relationship. After that nothing seemed the same. I would catch myself looking at her hands and wondering if she had ever done anything similar. I wanted to believe that Shae, someone I loved more than life itself, would never do that...but the more I thought on it, the less I was sure.

And now after three long years I was willingly accompanying her on a trip that very well might end up the same as before. She allowed me to stay in my clothes, looking less than presentable while she pulled on a button-up and kept her jeans on.

Even in such an outfit she was able to stop hearts. I couldn't help but watch her as we rode silently in the back of her car. She had a different driver than the one that took us from the museum, but that didn't surprise me. I had come to understand that she had an insane amount of people working for her, and I barely got to meet any of them.

When her dark gaze traveled to mine I couldn't help but blush and look away.

I wanted to keep the hateful defiant act going, but it was hard to after I got over my initial shock. After some thinking I had come to the conclusion that what had happened was water under the bridge and that was...probably just who Shae was as a person and I could take it or leave it.

She had changed over the last few years, even if I didn't like to admit it. I saw it last night for the first time, and then again today. It was behind the angry cloud that seemed to cling to her at times. It was a softness I didn't get to see before.

A part of me wanted to keep up the facade just to protect myself from being hurt again...but another smaller part whispered to me that the risk was worth it.

I felt a small cool metal slip into my palm followed by Shae's warm fingertips. I looked down to see a shiny penny placed in the middle of my palm.

I gave her a look but I could already hear her question behind the action. She had done this before too and it always endeared me. I slipped it into my jean pocket.

"You've changed," I said. "Not much, but enough for me to notice."

She rolled her eyes and stared out the window.

"Therapy will do that to you," she muttered, barely audible.

I let out a small giggle.

"Like you would ever," I said teasingly. "Trying to get you to talk about your feelings is like trying to separate the Texan from Caroline."

She only shot me a deadpan look, making me realize that she was serious.

"Fuck really?" I asked and leaned towards her. "How long? Do you still go?"

She let out a loud sigh and looked back out the window.

"It didn't last long," she admitted. "But it was right after you left. One of the reasons I didn't go find you."

Her ears and neck were starting to turn a bright red.

Shae actually went to a place where someone would psychoanalyze her and tell her everything she was doing wrong? That didn't seem very like her at all...but it made a warmth explode in my chest all the same.

"I bet they kicked you out for arguing with her," I said playfully. Shae kept looking out the window and I could feel the embarrassment radiating off her. "I had less than healthy coping mechanisms. I went to the bar almost every night, barely ate, was hell bent on destroying myself and hoped that you would come and get me and say that everything was a mistake." I swallowed thickly. "Then mom called me saying she needed to tell me and dad something...and everything went downhill from there."

When I looked back at her I found her watching me intently.

"Your father..."

"Left us and went to go take care of his new family," I said. "After mom died I stalked him for a bit but chickened out before I could do any real damage."

She nodded.

"That must have been painful," she murmured.

Not moments later the car stopped in front of a tall building that seemed to shine in the midday light. We were in an area that I had never been before and there were only a few people walking down the street. The streets were clearer than I had ever seen in New York during this time.

"Let's go," she said and climbed out of the car.

I followed her and tried to swallow the emotions that were raging through me. It felt like I would be taken to my knees by them.

I never meant to confide such things to her...but she did it first. I knew how much it must have pained her to admit something that she deemed so embarrassing, but it meant the world to me.

It made those questions whirl through my mind even stronger now.

"Do I know the person we are meeting?" I asked.

She continued forward into the building expertly weaving through the doors and down the first hallway.

"Yes," she said. "Though this time the playing field is different." She paused right outside a double door, her hand on the shining knob. "And there won't be a dead body."

I froze at her words.

"I thought you said you'd wait—"

"I changed my mind," she said in a clipped tone. "After this you can figure out if you still want the arrangement you promised in my office and know that you cannot have just one part of this and not the other."

One part of her, she meant.

"Let's see how it goes," I said with a tight smile on my face.

She nodded and pushed open the doors. Inside the small room was one large circular table with a window that overlooked the street outside. In the center of the table, with a bald man in a suit behind him, was Anton... The man who I once saw shoot someone in the head without so much as a blink. He had the same chilling blue eyes but now his hair was graying and there were wrinkles around his mouth that I didn't remember before.

His job must age him considerably, I thought to myself.

A smile pulled at his lips breaking his stone-like facade.

"Well look what the cat dragged in," he said in a slightly accented tone. "It's Jean right?"

"Yes it is," I said in a sweet tone. "Nice to see you again Anton."

"Such a sweet lie for this old man, I feel honored," he said and let out a huff that I assumed to be a chuckle. Shae pushed me forward with a steadying hand on my lower back.

"I thought it would be nice to liven up the brunch," Shae said in her usual playful tone. "Not like we have *important* matters to discuss."

Anton's lips twitched again.

When we sat down the doors opened back up immediately and we were served cups of hot tea.

"I did want to discuss rumors I heard," he said. "But merely just wanted to confirm the validity with you."

"Sure thing," Shae said. Her air of confidence was astounding; I was shaking as soon as his eyes passed over me.

"Rumors are you are doing business with someone who is harboring a trafficker," he said as the tip of his fingertip circled the edge of the tea cup. "You know how I feel about those people, especially when children are involved."

I froze but tried to act normal by taking a sip of the hot tea. It did nothing to calm my nerves.

"I am working on him now actually," she said. "Funny that you mention it. Who brought this to your attention?"

Anton shook his head with a smile.

"I do not reveal sources," he said. "But I am glad to hear you are working on it. When can we expect him to be *taken care of*?"

God, was Shae really going to kill this guy?

But this was a supposed human trafficker...one that deals in children. My stomach was almost sick thinking about it. Those people deserved worse than hell.

"Any day now," she said in a light tone, as if talking about the weather. "It seems to be a network and I want them all as far away from my contact and our goods as possible."

"Because I have your goods to look forward to in those ports, it would be a horrible loss if they opened the wrong shipment," he said, his tone dropping. It was a warning.

"I understand," Shae said and sent Anton a smile. "You know me Anton. How long have we been working together? I got this."

"Yet it took you months to find out," he noted.

The doors opened behind us once more and the smell of delicious food wafted through the room. I caught sight of a bunch of different meats, noodles, and pastries but they only made my stomach turn even more.

Once the staff was gone Shae let out a sigh.

"I already have arranged for the ports to be changed, and from there we can wash our hands of it," she assured.

Anton nodded.

"Same friend from the Matisse incident?" he asked.

"The exact same," she confirmed and made quick work of dividing up the food. She filled my plate first then went on to hers. Anton's gaze buried into mine.

"Sorry for such a heavy topic, my dear," he said. "I'm sure the thought of those children is a heavy one for you."

I nodded towards him and swallowed thickly before being able to speak.

"My heart aches for them," I admitted. "I hope this can be resolved soon."

Instead of filling his plate Anton just continued to look at me, then shifted his gaze towards Shae.

"What was his name again?" Anton asked. "We should meet, I would like to get to know the man who has saved our hide again and again."

Shae paused to drink some tea, then cleared her throat.

"I never gave you a name Anton, don't try to play me," she said, her tone hardening. "What is the push here?"

Anton finally moved to fill his plate, the clink of the utensils the only thing breaking the silence in the room.

"I just want to ensure my business with you is not a liability," he admitted. "Many of my partners have come to me begging to cut ties, but I assure them you are as good as they come."

Shae leaned forward.

"We wouldn't be sitting here if you had *real doubts*," she said. "I appreciate you flagging it to me though. Let me know if I can help with the pressure at all."

Anton shook his head and let out a small laugh.

"I got it," he said. "One even thought you were working with them when they saw you entering their main office. I should have shot him as soon as he insinuated anything."

"I did enter the office," Shae admitted. Her eyes shifted towards me for a second before going back to Anton. "But only to put some pressure on him. He caved soon after and met with our friend."

Anton nodded, "Let's change to a lighter subject, your lovely lady seems to be put off by this gruesome talk."

I shot Anton a grateful smile.

~

I DIDN'T SPEAK for the entire ride back. Hunter had texted me asking about my day but I couldn't bring myself to lie to him.

"Your ports seem to be a hot topic," I muttered as we stepped back into the sanctuary of her penthouse.

I always loved this place.

It was filled with the most wonderful art that just seem to radiate a sense of wonder while also being beautiful enough to draw the eye. When I looked at them I could always feel the rest of the world fall away with ease and my problems seemed minuscule in comparison.

Shae's hands began kneading the back of my neck and shoulder area. I leaned into her with a sigh.

"You did good," she said and I felt her place a kiss on the top of my head. "Have you thought about our deal?"

I leaned back and looked up at her, meeting her gaze. The small lines around her eyes were more strained now. She seemed to be tense.

"You could get any girl you wanted," I said with a bitterness I didn't mean to add. "Are *you* sure this is what you want?"

Her lips twisted into a familiar smirk. Her hand trailed from my shoulder around to my neck, applying light pressure and forcing my head back even further.

"I told you," she said her voice barely above a whisper. "I waited three years for you; I do not plan to take another."

My heart pounded in my chest so hard I swear she could hear it.

"Did you truly never take another?" I asked in a husky voice. This was it... The answer I was waiting for. The one I needed.

She leaned closer, her lips brushing my forehead as she spoke.

"I never have nor never will," she vowed. "After I met you I did not dare dream of anyone else but you."

I don't know who moved first but before I knew what happened, my hands were tangled in her hair and our mouths crashed together violently, teeth and all.

Her hands found their way to the back of my thighs and forced my legs around her waist. I moaned against her as our kiss deepened. She was so intoxicating. Every time her lips touched mine I was a goner, lost completely in her.

It wasn't just in the way she kissed me though, it was in everything she did. The way she held me, the way she watched me when she thought I wasn't looking. There was always something lurking behind her gaze and actions. It made me feel safe and protected and even though her job had its fair share of danger, she had shown me that *I* would never be in danger.

"I'm sorry I left," I said against her mouth. "I should have stayed and worked it out with you."

She smiled against me and pulled away only to dump me onto the couch and climb over my body.

"I knew you would come to your senses," she teased. As she looked down at me her hand came to brush a strand out of my face. "As mad as I was at you for leaving, it was for the best." She must have seen the hurt on my face because she quickly explained. "I had a lot of growing to do, I still do. But without you leaving I wouldn't have realized how horrible I was to you."

"Shae you were—"

She cut me off with a kiss to my mouth.

"I was horrendous to you. Immature. I couldn't even understand my own feelings. You were lightyears ahead of me in that regard," she admitted. Her eyes shifted and that red started to work up to her face once more. "But I know now that I—"

I cupped over her mouth with my hand.

"After I break up with him," I said quickly. "I don't want this to be spoiled by him. I want to be wholly yours when you say it."

Her eyes widened but she nodded against me and leaned down to kiss me. She was stopped short by the vibrating in my pocket.

She let out a loud sigh.

"Answer it," she said.

I fished out the phone and a sense of dread filled me when I saw Hunter's name flash across the screen. I met Shae's eyes and she just nodded to me.

"Hey, what's the matter?" I asked.

"Nothing's the matter babe," Hunter said in a tone that told me he was smiling. "I just wanted to keep you company on your lunch break."

"That's nice of you," I said. "But I don't want to take up your time."

A devious smirk crossed Shae's face and her fingers moved like lightning to undo the button on my jeans. My breath caught in my throat. She had done this before too but now I was on the one on the phone.

"Nah," Hunter replied. "I'm not doing anything interesting here anyways."

As Shae's hand slipped into my underwear I muted the phone.

"Be a good girl and keep your boyfriend entertained for me," she said with a smirk. Her thumb found my clit easily and I had to hold onto her shirt to keep myself from flying forward as intense pleasure shot through me. "On speaker."

"Babe?" Hunter asked. With a shaky breath I put him on speaker and unmuted myself.

"Sorry was talking to a coworker," I said trying to keep my

voice calm as Shae rubbed my clit and lazily played between my folds. I sunk into the couch, my limbs becoming jelly. "Tell me about your day."

Wrong. Wrong. Wrong, my brain screamed at me but it became quieter as Shae slowly entered two fingers into me. They slipped in so easily and I could already feel myself tightening around them.

As Hunter jumped into his monologue of his day I muted the call to let out a breathy moan.

"God Shae," I groaned as her fingers hooked inside me reaching a spot that made my toes curl. With her free hand she lifted up my hoodie and latched onto one of my nipples. I couldn't hold in the cry.

"Can you believe that?" Hunter asked drawing me back to the conversation. I unmuted myself quickly.

"I can't," I said shakily. Shae bit down on my nipple and forced her fingers to move faster inside me. "What are you g-going to do?"

"Are you okay?" he asks.

I closed my eyes and arch into Shae's mouth as she takes the other nipple into her mouth.

"Fine," I said quickly. "Just trying to focus on some last-minute work."

I felt a heat flare in my belly, building so fast that I almost didn't have enough time to mute the phone before I came with a shout.

"Unmute," Shae growled against my nipple then bit down on it. "I'm not done."

She's insatiable, I thought panicked. But truth be told, it was turning me on as well. Even as skilled as she was I could only remember a few other times I had come so fast. I unmuted like she asked.

"But I'm listening," I said interrupting him. "Keep going."

I moved to mute him again but Shae caught me and leaned forward, her lips brushing the shell of my ear.

"Keep it unmuted," she whispered. "And stay quiet while I fuck you with my tongue."

If I wasn't wet before I was drenched now. As if she realized it too her fingers flexed inside me.

"It's just like I don't know why father refuses to hire competent people," he complained. "They sit around and do nothing, I constantly have to clean up after them."

Shae removed my pants fully before lowering herself between them. Her eyes watched me even the whole time even as she dragged her tongue across the length of my slit.

I fought to keep in the gasp she then pulled away and raised her brow at me.

She was kidding right?

I shook my head at her and glared. She shrugged and began to pull away before I hooked my legs around her neck. She smirked and looked at me expectantly.

"Maybe you need to talk to him," I suggested and was rewarded with a soft suck to my clit. I arched back against the couch and used my free hand to push her face into me. She bit my thigh causing me to let out a yelp.

"Are you okay?" he asked. "Did you get hurt?"

"Just spilled something on me," I said. "Sorry go ahead."

This time when her mouth returned to me she began feasting on me like I was air and she couldn't breathe. Her tongue was everywhere teasing me in the right places and *oh god* when she sucked on my clit tears filled my eyes.

"You seem distracted babe," he said in a disappointed voice. "Maybe I should leave you to your work."

Thank god.

"Sorry ya, it's just a-a lot of wor—" I was cut off by her fingers entering me. "Of work. I'll talk to you when I get off."

"Sure babe, I lo—"

I hung up and threw my phone across the room. She began fucking me in earnest then, her hand pounding into me so hard I knew I would be left sore afterwards but I didn't care. With each thrust her thumb brushed my clit and I was pushed closer to my second orgasm.

"That was fucked," I gasped and gripped at the couch when I felt my body coil and heat flare deep in my belly. A string of curses left my mouth.

"You liked it," she said with a laugh. "You almost came twice. I should have fucked you harder." She pushed her hand into me harder as if to prove her point. "So he could hear you scream my name while you come."

That did it. The coil inside me snapped and I came so hard barely any noise came out of my lips. She continued her assault on me adding her mouth to my clit, throwing me into wave after wave of orgasm.

"*Please fuck*— Shae, no mor—" I was cut off by another orgasm ripping through me. Sobs wracked my body as I felt the blinding pleasure rack my body.

"You're done when I say you are," she growled against me. She pulled one more screaming orgasm out of me before she let my body collapse into the couch.

She climbed back up the couch only to lay me on my side and pull me to her. I curled into her warmth enjoying the feel of her against me finally. It felt like coming home after a long time. The scent, the feeling, was just as I remembered it.

"You have to stop doing that," I muttered. "It's embarrassing."

She chuckled and ran her hand through my hair.

"You can stop it anytime," she said. "You remember it right?"

"Yes," I grumbled.

"Say it," she said with a laugh. "So I know you know."

"...monkey balls," I whispered into her chest.

"What?" she asked. I knew she fucking heard it though because her whole body was shaking from her laughter.

"Monkey balls!" I yelled at her and looked up at her with a glare.

There was a rare smile across her face that made my heart skip a beat. Her face looked so lively, so unburdened. I leaned forward and captured her lips. In this moment I had never wanted to touch her more. My hand trailed up her torso but she stopped me with a laugh.

"Those rules are still the same," she said and pulled away. "Maybe we can work up to it."

I raised my brow.

"Really?"

She nodded.

"For you, I will try anything," she said. "But don't get mad when I end up fucking you until you can't even move."

I rolled my eyes.

"You're all talk," I egged on. Her eyes lit up.

"Bet," she said and captured my lips once more.

Jean

It was harder than I thought to tear myself away from her. I wanted to stay in our bubble forever and forget the world outside, but I knew what I had to do.

The drive back to my apartment was over far too quickly and I found myself hesitating outside of my door. It was five o'clock and I knew Hunter would be home soon, if not already waiting for me behind this door.

This was it. I had made my bed and now I had to lie in it. And truth be told, Hunter and I were just not compatible from the start. I was trying too hard to forget her and Hunter was the perfect person to do that with.

This whole thing wasn't fair to him and I at least owed it to him to end this before he actually proposed.

With a last deep breath I opened the door and entered my apartment. Hunter was already sitting at the bar area. He looked up with a small smile as I came in.

"Hey babe," he greeted. "How was work?"

I closed the door behind me and gave him a hesitant smile.

"Um, I wanted to talk to you about some stuff," I said and moved to sit with him at the bar. He raised a brow at me but I just shook my head.

"Are you okay?" he asked in a sincere voice.

"I'm fine it's just…"

"If it's about your job, I already know," he said casually and lifted the glass of water. "But didn't want to embarrass you by saying anything."

Shock flooded through me and I could feel my face heating.

"How did you find out?" I asked.

"Did you like the present I left you?" he asked ignoring my question.

I cocked a brow at him.

"The present?"

"You're not very good at hiding things," he tsked. The smile had dropped from his face at that point and his eyes drifted towards mine. There was something behind them that didn't sit right with me. "Like the escorting."

In an instant, it all clicked.

"It was *you,*" I gasped and took a step back.

"Oh don't act so dramatic," he drawled. His hazel eyes narrowed on me and I felt a chill travel up my spine.

I was at a loss for words.

Hunter? Why would he do that?

"Why?" I asked. I had so much more to say but that was the only thing that seemed to escape my lips.

He waved his hand and took a sip of his water.

"It didn't bother me that much," he said. "The escorting."

"Then why, Hunter?" I asked. "Why would you purposefully make me lose my only legit source of income?"

He let out a small huff of a laugh and shook his head. His curly locks fell into his face, shielding his expression from view.

"The ex-girlfriend gave you more than enough by the looks of it," he said. He turned his face so I could fully see his expression. His face was slack except for the dangerous narrowing of his eyes. The hair on the back of my neck stood up and my whole body was telling me to bolt…

But this was *Hunter.* He was harmless.

"That's actually what I wanted to talk about," I confessed trying to regain control of this conversation. There was a cloud hanging over us and each minute it seemed to darken. "And us."

He sat back and dropped his gaze back to the glass.

"Was it the sex?" he asked. "Was it not good enough? Because there is nothing else I can think of."

I shifted uncomfortably in my seat.

"We just aren't right for each other," I said. "We want different things in life."

He let out a harsh laugh.

"I was going to marry you," he said. "Do you understand how good of a life you could have had?"

"It's not about a good life, Hunter," I said. "It's about a happy one. I'm sorry, I never expected to want to go back to her but I knew in my heart that you and I could just never work out."

"Was that before or after she tongued you in my parents' house?" he asked harshly. The breath was taken out of me.

"How did you—"

"Or was it before then?" he asked. "When you were escorting with... What's his name? Berry?"

"Gary," I corrected. "Have you been watching me?"

My pounding heart seemed to nestle its way into my throat, blocking the air to my lungs and causing a dizziness to cloud my brain.

He gave me an exasperated look.

"Of course I have been."

His confession shocked me to my core. This was not the person I knew, not the same person who had been there for me as I grieved my mother. Not the sweet man who had been here for every early morning and late night seeing me through the tough times when money was scarce.

"How long?"

He looked up to the ceiling then his eyes descended on me.

"For a year and a half," he admitted. "If you count our time together."

I stilled.

"You need to leave," I demanded. "I don't know what you are playing but I don't want any part of it."

He nodded and looked back to the glass.

"My guys spotted you and thought you would be a good addition to our product line," he said. "Your mom was dying soon, dad off with a new family, and you were sexy as hell. It didn't matter if you were old, I was sure I could find someone to pay well for you."

I gripped my phone in my pocket and moved to stand but Hunter's large hand pushed me back onto the stool.

"What are you talking about, Hunter? I met you when my mom died," I said remembering distinctively the handsome man that handed me a bottled tea as I was crying my eyes out.

"But then," he continued with a sigh. "I saw those tear-filled eyes and just couldn't help but take you for myself. Father wouldn't be happy that I married someone of your status, but you could play a part well... I had seen you do it when you thought people weren't looking and knew that I needed someone like you by my side." He stood and gripped my chin harshly forcing me to look at him. "It would have been the perfect cover, if you weren't such a whore."

I didn't have time to react, only watch as he lifted the glass still filled with water and brought it down against my head. I felt a searing pain explode inside me before the world went dark.

WHEN I CAME to next I was in a damp dark place and I couldn't feel my hands. There was a sharp pain in the side of my head and I couldn't help the groan that came out of my mouth.

"Finally." Hunter's voice came from somewhere a few paces in front of me. I had to blink a few times for my vision to finally clear but when I did I realized that I was in an enclosed space that was no bigger than the living room of my apartment.

His voice bounced off the walls as did his steps as he stalked forward.

He looked the same but now I understood that the glint in his eyes that I mistook for something sweet and innocent was not that way any longer.

"What the fuck did you do?" I growled at him.

He came to kneel in front of my knees. Only then did I realize that I was sitting and bound to the chair underneath me. My hands were behind my back and I would bet the reason the feeling in my fingers had left was because that *motherfucker* tied me to the chair.

As he came close I tried to headbutt him but he merely leaned back with a laugh.

"I thought that we could have a little chat," he said in a light tone. He brought out his phone and the screen lit up his face instantly. He turned it towards me and I had to squint to make it out.

It was a picture of me talking to Nick in the cafe where we bumped into each other at. I was smiling faintly in the picture and Nick smiled back at me.

"What?" I asked, my voice close to hysterics. "What does Nick have to do with this?"

Hunter's smile didn't drop as his hand connected with my cheek. My entire face snapped to the right and the chair tipped from the impact. The air was sucked out of me and immediately tears welled up in my eyes. Hunter reached into his pocket and pulled out a small pocket knife which he opened then used to tap the phone screen.

"Why were you talking to the FBI?" he asked. "Did you set me up?"

The fucking business card, I cursed internally. *I should have taken it.*

"What?" I asked. "I have no idea what you're talking about. Hunter what the fuck happened to you. This better be some kind of sick jok—"

He backhanded the other cheek cutting me off mid-sentence.

"Don't play dumb," he said in a sweet voice. "You may be a dirty whore but you are not a stupid one. What did you say to him?"

I swallowed the blood that filled my mouth. I had thought to spit it at him but I knew my chances were better if I was nice to him.

"He ran into me in the coffee shop that's it," I answered honestly.

"And where did you go after that, hm?" he asked as he trailed the knife up my jeans.

"I think you know where," I answered hoarsely.

His head tilted to the side and he added light pressure onto my thigh, the knife cutting into my skin slightly.

"Say it," he growled. The smile was now gone.

"I was with Shae!" I cried as the knife began cutting into my skin.

"See that wasn't so hard," he cooed. "And did Shae say anything about her involvement with the FBI?"

"Like she would be involved with them," I spat. After replaying the conversation with Anton in my head over and over again I knew that there was a possibility that she could be working with Nick in that capacity, but there was no way I would tell him that. "You know what she does, that would be like a death sentence."

"Not if he's dirty," Hunter said and pulled away the knife before standing. He looked down on me as if he was disgusted and I was nothing more than a bug under his shoe. "Your buyers will be here in an hour, be good until then."

My heart sank into my stomach and I could feel the bile rising up in my throat.

"Wait!" I called before he could leave. "Were you doing this the whole time? Was any of it real?"

He cocked a brow at me.

"Real?" he scoffed. "I needed you to keep up appearances

only. Nothing from our meeting until now has been real. I had such great plans, they would have made you so happy... But now that Shae fucked everything up you only have her to blame."

"It's not her that has me locked in a box," I growled.

He shook his head and laughed. This disgusting vile man was the same one that Shae had been trying to get out of her ports and the same one the FBI was trying to catch.

Who would have thought that someone like him was so adept at fooling everyone around him?

"I should have done this from the start," he said. "It was my bad that I got blinded by that ass of yours." He sighed. "But don't worry, you won't be missed and I am sure your new owners will take care of you *very well.*"

"I didn't know you could be so heinous," I muttered. "What happened to you Hunter? You were such a good kid."

Hunter smiled before backing away to push open the door to the small box. When the sea air filtered in I realized where I was.

"I was never a good kid," he said. "I was just good at pretend-ing." His eyes glanced over mine before giving me a chilling smile.

"Kind of like you."

With that I was left in the dark.

Shae

The sun had already begun setting over the city when I got a bad feeling. It started at the base of my spine and slowly crawled its way onto my shoulder before it put my neck into a chokehold. I had only felt fear like this once in my life and it had been so strong that even years later I could still feel the same ice-cold claw that sunk itself into my chest.

That was the only warning I got before the call came. It was from a number I didn't recognize and normally I would reject such calls, but this one felt different. I held it up to my ear without answering.

"Bidding starts at five hundred thousand," Hunter's voice said through the phone. "I have two other people here in line for the product."

"So now we are finally being honest with each other, are we?" I quickly put him on speaker and went into my office to check his phone. The air was still hot and Jean's scent invaded my senses once more.

Speaking of which, I thought. *Shouldn't she have texted me or something by now?*

"I never lied about what I was into," he said. "Just merely withheld the truth. Something you know all too well."

"I'm not bidding on a human life," I told him. His messages didn't tell me anything and it also wasn't the phone he called me on now. I tried to put his current number into the software my contact created for me but it froze.

"Oh man," he said in an overly exaggerated tone. "Jean will be upset to hear that."

My fingers froze over the keyboard.

"You didn't," I growled back at him.

The fury that rose in me was nothing like I had felt before. It was potent and felt like my insides were literally burning. I jumped into action pulling up Jonson's contact information and sent him a message with the phone number Hunter was calling from.

"I did," he said with a chuckle. "And if you pay me I'll let her go. But if not I'll give her to my friends here and they can have their way with her." I heard a clanging in the background. "Normally someone her age and so worn would be hard to sell...but these people like it rough so they will take almost any piece of meat you throw their way."

"What is your motive?" I asked. "Are you really that mad that I took her from you?"

Jonson messaged saying he had a location and would go over right now. I wanted to let out a sigh but the feeling that had a chokehold around my throat was not gone yet.

"Not at all," he said. "I just wanted to use her to avoid suspicion but when I saw *your contact* talking to her this morning... things started clicking into place."

"I don't know what you are talking about," I lied.

"Oh but you do," he said. "But if you *really* don't want to pay up—"

"I'll do it," I said quickly. "I can have the money in less than thirty and meet you wherever you need me."

Jonson was already on his way so maybe it would be done by the time I got there, but if not...

I reached into the desk to gather the handgun that had been

collecting dust in there. I wouldn't hesitate to use this. Just as my fingers were typing to Anton for backup, Hunter interrupted me.

"It's gone up to seven hundred now," he said. "And don't be stupid and bring your friends, I'll know."

I gritted my teeth.

"I don't have friends," I said. "Give me the address, I'll get you the money."

"Check your phone," he said. "Get here in thirty or I ship her off to the other buyers."

He hung up before I could answer and my phone dinged with a text from him not a moment later. The address was less than twenty minutes from here and it would give me more than enough time to get there and find Jean before he even knew what hit him.

I was never the person who was on the ground doing the dirty work—besides the stalking of course—but I would do it for Jean. I didn't care what I had to do, but I would stop at nothing until I got her back.

We were *so close,* to getting things on track and then this sick fuck thinks he can just come in here and take it all?

I should have taken her away from him sooner than this but I was too wrapped up in the thrill of the game while trying to balance her wants and needs.

I grabbed my keys, secured my gun, and left without grabbing the stash of money that was hidden under the floorboard of my closet.

THE PLACE he sent me to was a small port that I had only seen once before when I first started doing business with Carter. I had waved it off completely due to its size and now it felt like it was laughing and saying, "*HA! Look who is important now!*"

I had parked three blocks down and walked here in the shadows. I didn't see any armed men so I assumed the coast was clear.

The port was so small that there were only two large ships that could be stationed at one time but that didn't stop them from filling the yard to the brim with shipping containers.

I memorized the block number and container he sent me so it didn't take me long to find the area he had mentioned for me to meet him at. The air had a chill in it and the scent of salt water filled my senses. Even as my heart pounded and I began to sweat, I still pulled my jacket close to me.

I do not know if it was the cold or my fear that caused my teeth to chatter and my hands to shake but by the time the container was in sight I could hear the chattering of my teeth cut through the silence.

I stopped in my tracks when I heard a set of voices.

"Relax dude," a younger voice said. "Just take a hit, they won't even notice."

There was a pause before I heard a sigh and then a click of a lighter. I moved silently around the container and peered over the side to see both of their backs towards me. They both had hand-guns strapped onto their sides.

Small guns for such a job, I noted.

They lingered for only another minute before they walked further into the yard and in the opposite direction of where I was headed.

Hang on, Jean, I begged in my mind. She was probably scared out of her mind and I couldn't help but wonder if Hunter had already hurt her. I wouldn't put it past him given his inclination to preying on innocent young girls.

When I knew for sure that the hired arms were far enough away, I snuck past the crates searching for number 7812. As I passed each container my heart pounded louder and louder in my chest. I just imagined what he was doing to her in that crate all alone, how pissed he was, and I regretted pushing him so hard before this. It was my fault we were in this situation and now I had to figure a way out of this that guaranteed both of our safety.

I let out a sigh of relief when I found the container. I listened carefully, stopping myself from running straight towards it. There was no sound, not even a rustle beyond the metal doors.

This should have been a good sign. Should have told me that Jean was safe in there and like he promised, was waiting for me to come get her.

But none of it eased my panic. Instead it only fueled it and I found my legs racing towards the metal box without so much of an ounce of hesitation.

All I could think of was the image of her in there, bleeding out and crying silently as she waited for me to come and save her.

My shaking hands found the lever to open it when a voice shook me out of my panic-filled haste.

"Do you really think I'm that stupid?" Hunter's voice echoed out from behind me. I turned to look at the fucker, seeing red. He was flanked by the two guards I had passed earlier, both of their arms raised and guns pointed right at my face.

I held my hands up and tried to put on an easy smile even though I wanted nothing more than to attack him right there as he stood and wipe that smug look off his face.

"Had to try," I said easily, pretending like I wasn't losing my god damn fucking mind. "Let me see her and I'll give you the money."

Hunter rolled his eyes and gave me an exasperated look. I *hated* how much control he had over me right now and felt myself losing control. I tried to reign myself in but not for me...at least for Jean. If I died here she would be stuck with this monster.

"You're carrying awfully light to have brought the money with you," he noted. "Did you go back on our deal?"

He motioned for the men at his side and they took a step closer towards me, their gazes locked.

"No," I lied quickly. "The money is in a bag near my car. I want to see her first before anything happens."

"I didn't kill her," he said. "My guys will go get your money and bring it here. Then I will count it and you can be on your way."

"Sure," I said. "While they are gone you can show me Jean. I don't believe you when you say you won't hurt her."

"Nah, I think I'll wait," he said and motioned for the guys to leave. Much to my dismay only one guy left, leaving me outnumbered.

"You really think I would have let you talk all that shit?" he asked, probably noticing my jumpiness. He was using this to egg me on.

"I didn't talk shit," I replied. "Just called it like I saw it."

I knew I fucked up when his jaw twitched.

"You think you are in the position to fight me right now?" he asked.

I gritted my teeth and bit my tongue. Now was not the time to act out.

He hummed and smirked, satisfied with my lack of response.

We waited the rest of the time in silence as the man was off to find my car. Hunter looked calm and collected, so did the man next to him even as he held a gun to my face. I on the other hand was sweating bullets...because the car he went to had absolutely no money in it.

And when they found it we were both dead.

I tried to think of a way to get out of this. Of a way to escape... but that damn guard's eyes never left mine even as his boss started to lazily pace around the area.

I fucked up, I realized. I should have at least brought something, but I didn't think they would catch me so fast. This whole god damn time I was acting so invincible and it landed me in hot water.

Where the fuck was Jonson?

Hunter's phone rang and with it my heart sank. He gave me a smile before answering it. He was silent as he looked over me and listened to whoever was on the other end. I couldn't hear the caller from our distance, but I could guess what he was saying.

Hunter's smile dropped and he slowly strode towards me, his lackey following him closely behind. He slowly ended the call and shoved it into his pocket with a loud exaggerated sigh. His hazel eyes caught mine once more before, like lightning, he held a pocket knife to my neck, pushing the tip of it just enough into my skin to sting.

"You must really not want to live," he drawled, a crazed smile tugging at his lips. "I wanted to do this so bad when you came into my office that day, do you remember it? The way you sat at my desk and acted like you were hot shit. Who would have thought it would end up like this?"

This was the real Hunter. The one with a glint in his eyes. The one who giggled under his breath like he just won the lottery. All of it started to make sense now.

The real psychopath had been hiding behind this mask and *finally* he was free to shed his skin and show the world what a real monster he was.

The realization shook me to my core, and not because my life was being held together by a string. No, because I realized that no matter what happened...he would not be leaving here until he was satisfied and that meant one of us had to die.

I tried to lower my hands but the guy behind Hunter only cocked his gun at the action. Hunter pushed the knife into the thin skin of my throat hard enough for the blood to pool and run down my neck. I winced at the pain.

"Just let me see Jean," I pleaded. "A dying wish, if you will."

I had to think of something fast or else this crazy bitch really would kill me.

"Open the crate," he commanded to the guy behind him but his eyes never left mine.

The boy nodded and lowered his gun before putting it back in his holster. When he passed me to open the crate he glared at me. I wanted to roll my eyes at him but I was in no state with a knife to my throat. Hunter's breathing was scarily calm even though his eyes looked crazed under the dull lights.

I heard the crate open but did not turn just yet.

"Well take a look," Hunter said, his voice strangely excited. He lifted the knife just enough so I could turn and face the container.

My heart stopped in my chest and I felt my eyes sting. I balled my hands into fists ready to destroy the man, because in front of me was a container that held but a single red rose.

Every single hope and dream that I had with Jean crumbled right before my eyes. We would never live the life together that we were desperately fighting for. There would be no more after this and I desperately held on to the last moments that I had seen her.

I couldn't get her smiling face out of my mind as I kissed her perfect lips.

Or the way she giggled as I tickled her in bed.

Or the way she woke up in the morning with her hair sticking up on all sides of her head.

And she would never know that I loved her.

She was the only person that I truly loved.

The only person that saw me...and I was too immature to handle it.

And now she would never know... It broke my heart to think that whatever happened after this...she would never know my true feelings and all she would remember was the monster that pushed her away and into this life of darkness.

Hunter's knife dug into my throat once more.

"I never planned to give her back to you," he said. "I plan to keep her locked in a dark place where no one will ever find her again and only visit her when I need to wet my dick. That's the only life she will know after this and it's all *thanks to you and that fucking FBI—*"

A shot rang through the still night air and all I could think about was how this was karma coming to get me.

There was a cold that had sunken through the metal confines of this space and straight into my bones. The sweatshirt and jeans I had been wearing previously did nothing to help me in this state, making shivers wrack my body. The chair I was tied to in the middle of the dark space remained steady and kept me confined in this place.

It was just me and my thoughts in here and that almost terrified me just as much as what awaited me.

It took all but ten minutes to figure out that I would probably be stuck here until Hunter finds me the "owners" he was talking about. It was almost comical how this all turned out and I couldn't do anything but wait like a sitting duck.

I was wrapped like a fucking present to them, I thought pitifully.

I wasn't strong by any means but I would fight like hell before I let those disgusting humans take me.

My gut twisted painfully when I realized how Hunter had hidden this entire world from me all this time. Here he was running what I could only assume to be an empire of a business all while putting on that sweet facade. The men that I caught glances of and the way he talked about the people he dealt with... There was no way this was a new venture for him.

How could someone as sweet and kind as him turn into...this horrible person? I had thought that the person who had made me breakfast, the person who had helped me through my mother's death, could not possibly be the same person as the one who just locked me in here.

"I fucking attract these goddamn people," I muttered and let out a loud groan.

I believed Hunter was the break I needed, a break from the craziness of Shae and her underground world. I knew that I wasn't built for this life from the start, even as I was escorting. For god's sake, I lost my lunch when I thought of the man that was murdered right in front of me.

I may have been able to put on a brave face and *act* the part... but that's all it was.

Tugging once again at the ropes that bound my wrists, tears stung my eyes. The ropes had long since bit into my skin and the area began to burn. By the wet feeling running down my numbing hand, I guessed they were bleeding.

The room was mostly dark save for the small hole in the ceiling. It let the moonlight seep in but only in the single corner right near the entrance. It was enough to calm my racing mind and scare away *some* of the nastier thoughts that threatened to pull me into a spiraling panic...but it wasn't enough for me to determine my own state.

At least they have the decency to make sure I don't suffocate, I thought bitterly.

My body was aching all over and I knew that they had been rough with me while I slept, but that wasn't the main concern and I wouldn't let it slow me down as I tried for my escape. I needed to get these binds off and make a run for it.

I tried again to pull my hands off the tight rope, but it only resulted in a painful burning sensation that shot up my arms. I let out a whimper.

My mind told me to give up, and to wait for rescue... But sitting here in the dark with the laps of the waves against something in the distance, it became clear that no one except Hunter knew that I was out here.

No one would be coming for me, so I couldn't give up now even if my body begged me to stop.

With that drive in mind, I continued to pull until I felt just an inch of my hand pull out of the rope.

A small spark of hope lit in my chest and I steadied myself before pulling against the rope harder this time. I bit my lip to stop the loud groan from escaping from my mouth in hopes that whatever guards were out there, if there were any, would not hear me in my plan to get out of here.

After I got the rope over my knuckles I slipped my hand out with ease and turned to the other knot, only to pause as I heard a voice outside the metal walls of the container.

It was muffled but the good news was that even after a few minutes sitting utterly still in the darkness, I only heard a single voice.

Hunter was always a stupid one, I thought smugly. Though I didn't let myself get too cocky. After all, I was in here with nothing but a chair and didn't even know how to get out of here.

When the voice died down I tried the knot again but it was almost impossible to undo with one hand. Sighing, I looked around in the darkness to locate something—*anything*—to help me out of this chair but again... I was disappointed.

Then an idea hit me that was so *stupid* that I thought for sure it would fail, but I refused to be a quitter. Not after everything that I had been through. This shit of a life had fucked me over one too many times for me to give up right now. I deserved to get out of here and make my life what I wanted.

"God I hope this works," I muttered before screaming at the top of my lungs.

I had screamed before when they first left me in here, but it was angry, full of rage. I had cursed Hunter and his entire soul, but this time I filled it with fear.

It pierced the air and was deafening as it bounced off the metal walls.

"No! Don't come closer!" I yelled and rocked back and forth on my chair. "Ah! Please help me!"

I heard the fiddling with the door before my screams even ended. I quickly positioned my wrist back behind my chair so they wouldn't see my little project and put on an expression full of fear.

When the door opened, moonlight filtered through and I got a good look at the guy who had been standing outside my cell.

He was *young*.

So young it made my heart ache for him. How had he gotten in this? I couldn't help but imagine that he was somewhat like me... A person who was brought to dirty jobs in order to make a living and just so happened to get involved with a monster like Hunter.

"You made me think someone was in here," he complained with a slight drawl. His hand was fastened to the holster on his right side. A light feeling fluttered in my chest when I saw the gun.

"Behind me!" I squeaked and rocked the chair again. "It's a snake!"

The boy's eyes widened before looking back outside. We both knew that he shouldn't be in here, but now was the time to sell it.

"Please help!" I yelled even louder. His eyes shot back to the door and he sighed before walking over. "Over there! It's near my leg!"

I jerked my head to the side of my free arm. He was in front of me now. I tried to peer up at him with puppy dog eyes.

"I don't see anything," he muttered and bent to the side. He removed the hand from the holster to steady himself on my chair as he was looking for the imaginary snake.

As fast as my shaky hand could manage, I reach forward and grabbed the gun out of its holster and pushed it against his chest.

"One wrong move and I kill you where you stand," I threatened.

From this angle, the light hit his face just right so I could see the sides of his lips twitch.

"The safety is on you *idiot*," he growled and his hand slowly moved to grasp the hand that was holding the gun. His eyes trailed down the length of my face and I grimaced as his breath washed over me.

Pausing for just a moment, I made the quick decision to bring my forehead straight into his face.

He jerked back with a yell, leaving me with the gun. Squinting in the dim light I tried to make out the switch for the safety. I had only seen someone do this once in my lifetime and now it seemed an impossible task.

My fingers fumbled and the gun clattered to the ground. There was a pause as the man and I slowly looked towards each other. The gun was out of my reach, we both knew that, but that didn't stop me from flinging my entire weight forward and stretching out my free hand. I fell to the ground with a thud but he was already there, his foot stomping down onto my outstretched hand.

I could feel the cool metal of the gun brush across my fingertips.

This was it, I thought as the weight of what was happening bore down on me. *These were my last moments on earth.*

Even if I was able to live through this, it would probably still be at the hands of these dirty people. The same people that sold young girls, and only god knows what they did to them. Soon, I would be one of them.

Shae's rare smiling face flashed across my mind.

Would I ever see her again?

I had left her ready to end it all, ready to come back into her arms and start our lives over. I had dreams of our future. The future that we never had together.

It had taken me so long to realize that no matter what she did, or how dangerous it was...that I would never stop coming back to her. She had known that all along, it was only I who was so blinded by the bad parts in our relationship that I overlooked everything else.

I had never asked her *why* she couldn't tell me she loved me.

I never asked *why* she had to constantly be on the move.

I never asked *why* she had chosen me and made her talk through those feelings.

Instead I was so utterly selfish that I just left everything instead of trying to focus on what mattered. I could have done so much for her, but instead I just took and took and never tried to find out what was behind that cold mask of hers.

He bent down to pick up the gun. The cool metal was pulled away from my fingertips and it took my hope with it.

"Please," I whispered and strained my neck to look up at him. "Let me go."

"Why would I do that?" he asked and cocked his head to the side. "I'm getting paid to do this, sweetheart."

"You can't possibly enjoy this," I choked out. Tears finally spilled over and ran down my face. "You're young, you have your whole life—"

He put more weight on the foot that was crushing my arm and twisted his foot. I let out a gargled moan at the action.

"Shut up," he spit at me. "Don't test me."

"Hands up!" a voice yelled from the open door of the crate.

A violent relief crashed through me when I saw Nick's familiar face in the moonlight. He held a gun towards the man standing above me.

The man let out a sigh before he pointed the gun directly at me.

"No witnesses," he growled.

There was ringing so loud in my head that I could feel it bounce off the walls of my skull. Time seemed to slow and all I could see was the man's snarl above me as he lifted the gun.

I'm sorry Shae, I thought. *I really did love you.*

I closed my eyes and waited for the blow. The sound of the gun firing off in such a small space caused me to flinch.

It was then, that I realized I was still alive. I opened my eyes to see the once snarling man above me sway and then take a step back, before collapsing on the floor.

Nick rushed towards me, running straight past the man. As he hauled my chair up I got an eyeful of the blood that was pouring out of the man's chest wound. By the way his eyes were glazed over I knew that he was most likely dead.

Nick set to undoing the knots from around my ankles and wrists.

"How did you...?" I asked trying to tear my eyes away from the body.

"Shae sent me," he confessed.

A flurry of excitement and panic rushed through me. If she was here that meant that she would also come face to face with Hunter.

"We have to get her!" I rushed out. "Hunter he—"

"He is in custody," he said from my side as he undid the knot on my right hand. I rubbed the sore area as he moved on to the next one.

"But where is—"

"Jean!" Shae's voice sounded and not a moment later she rushed into the small container. Her black hair was a mess around her head and even in the cold weather, she was sweating buckets.

Just as Nick undid the last of the knots I shot towards her and ran into her open arms. She pulled me into a tight hug and exhaled shakily.

"This is a crime scene!" Nick yelled.

Shae's hands found the side of my face and she brought her lips to mine. The kiss ignited a warmth inside me that made my already weak knees buckle.

"I thought I would never see you again," I said against her lips.

"I am here now," she said without pulling away. "You will *never* have to deal with this ever again I promise you—"

"Get out!" Nick yelled and I felt his hands push us towards the exit. "She has to get checked by medical and Shae you have to get the hell out of here."

Shae lifted me and pulled us out of the metal prison. Watching her now, the tension of the incident fell off of me and a violent relief crashed through me. Sobs racked my chest and I buried my face into her damp shirt, unable to hold on to my sanity any longer.

People were moving around us, I could feel and hear them but I focused only on the warmth that Shae was emitting. I inhaled her familiar scent through my gasps.

"Shae I—"

"I need to examine her," a soft male voice interrupted.

"You need to leave," Shae growled above me.

"Please, miss, she is bleeding," the man said in a soft tone.

Shae paused and with shaky movements I lifted my head to look her in the eyes. She had a frown on her face. Her eyes drifted down my face and to the hand that grasped her shirt. I had known that I had done a number on my wrist. My stomach clenched as I saw the broken and bleeding flesh.

That would leave a nasty scar, I thought.

"Will you be okay?" Shae asked me. I took a few deep breaths, calming my sobs before nodding. I looked over towards the soft-spoken man. He met me with a kind smile.

"She can stay with you as I patch you up but they will probably require a statement afterwards," he warned and stepped back to motion us forward.

Only then did I notice the chaos the area was in. I had guessed that we were at some shipping center but rows and rows of containers awaited us and in between them were teams of people in uniforms, cop cars, and multiple ambulances.

I swallowed thickly and hid in Shae's chest as she followed the man to one of the ambulances.

"Why are there so many?" I asked in a whisper.

"They are here to rescue the others," the man said as he

reached into the back of the ambulance, pulling out his equipment. "Over ten crates have been found with women and children in them."

Shae made a noise of disgust as she sat me down on the edge of the ambulance. She still remained close, as if afraid to leave me.

I reveled in the thought, a selfish part of me ate up every ounce of attention and love she was giving me.

"Are they okay?" I croaked. "I never knew Hunter..."

I trailed because I had no words for this monster. How could someone be so vile as him?

"Leave that talk for the statement," Shae said and stepped back. "Jonson would kill me if he figured I heard your statement first."

The medic lightly grabbed my wrist, pulling my attention from Shae to him. I gave him a sheepish look.

"I may just be a medic," he murmured. "This will hurt." I winced at the pain from the disinfectant he used on my wound. "But I have to agree with her. Protect yourself."

I swallowed thickly and chose to remain silent for the rest of the time. Shae watched me intently, only moving to grab my free hand and massaging the tender area of my wrist. That moment alone spoke volumes.

We were interrupted by a woman in a suit before the medic was even done wrapping my wound. She had a hard expression and looked at Shae with visible disgust.

"Cheryl," Shae greeted with a twist of her lips.

"Scram, Shae," she replied. "I have a few questions for your *friend.*"

"She's my partner," Shae corrected glaring at the woman before looking towards me. "Call me if you need anything, I'll be over there," she said pointing through the flashing lights and to where Nick stood talking to a uniformed cop with an angry expression. I nodded and turned towards the woman.

"I am sure you have a lot of ques—"

"I don't," I interrupted feeling a pang as Shae walked further away. "Can we get this over with?"

She let out a sigh before she began shooting out rapid-fire questions.

I could barely pay attention to the questions or my responses to them. I was busy staring at Shae as she continued to watch me. I had so much that I wanted to say to her.

I love you.

I am sorry.

I should have been better.

And so much more...but I didn't know where to start. I wanted to spill everything and anything I could to her. Have her take me back to the penthouse and wrap me up in our favorite blanket and vow to never come out again.

But the question was, would she even want me after this?

When Cheryl was done with the questioning the medic had cleaned and bandaged all my wounds without so much as a word. Only when she turned to leave did he smile at me softly.

"You are all set," he said. "I am sorry this happened to you and wish you the best with you and your partner."

My face felt hot but I muttered a thank you nonetheless.

"Are you done?" Shae asked walking up with Nick at her side. Disappointment filled my gut. I wanted just a moment alone with her but it would seem everyone was hell-bent on interrupting our reunion.

"All set," I said in a small voice and sent her a forced smile.

Her eyes lit up and that signature smirk spread across her face. Even after all that had happened and how bad I had felt in the moment, that smirk caused butterflies to free themselves in my stomach.

She leaned down and placed her hands on either side of me, pushing her face mere inches from mine. Without warning she crashed her lips to mine so forcefully that I had to fling my arms around her shoulders to stop myself from falling backwards.

She used this as a chance to loop her hand around me and

push on the small of my back, forcing me closer to her. Ignoring the throbbing pain in my wrists I melted into her and deepened the kiss.

I heard Nick's throat clearing but we both ignored it, focusing only on each other. The kiss was passionate, and everything it had been once before but there was something else there... A raging fire that had seemed so small before that now consumed us.

It was her that pulled away first.

"I love you, Jean," she said against me in a heated tone. "I was so stupid before, please forgive me."

"No!" I said panicked. "I should be sorry! I never gave you a chance to—"

"Jean," she said with a sigh. "I am trying to tell you—"

"Oh my god!" Nick exclaimed from behind us. "If you two don't get over yourselves and get out of my crime scene I will have you both arrested."

Shae and I both paused and looked over to a stunned Nick. His face was turning a bright red and I couldn't help the laugh bubbling inside my throat.

Turning back to Shae I smiled and said, "I love you too."

The smile she gave me was unlike any I'd seen and I knew in that moment that I would remember her like this forever. Even as we aged and turned into older, greyer versions of ourselves... I would never forget how she looked in this moment.

"Let's go home," she said.

Epilogue

THREE YEARS LATER

It was fall again and the air outside the city seemed much colder as I climbed out of the toasty car. After the incident I never could feel safe in the cold, but being so far outside the city with nothing but our house and silence... I found myself reveling in the comfort the winter provided.

The house that stood in front of us was a two-story three-bed-and-bath house that had been on the market a mere week before we had taken the plunge to buy it. The penthouse was great, but there got to be a time where we needed some fresh air and as soon as Shae had pulled up this property I fell in love.

It had a patio, beautiful white trimming and a light blue coat of paint that just seemed to blend in with the freshly fallen snow. It was a dream and something that I could have never dreamed of to afford...but here it was right in front of me, and it was all *ours*.

"Are you sure we can only stay here for a week?' I asked and pouted towards Shae as she rounded the front of the car.

She was wearing a black jacket and dark jeans, standing in stark contrast to the white environment behind her. Her hair was slicked back though she had chosen recently to grow it just a bit longer than she had in the past, so it curled behind her ears. I liked this style on her, showed a softer side than everyone was used to.

She sent me a smile and came to wrap her arm around my shoulder.

I let out a sigh and leaned into her comforting warmth.

"I have work," she said, then her eyes shifted from the house to me. "And so do you."

I let out a small laugh.

After Shae and I reconciled we had a serious talk about the future and what we wanted to do with our life together. One of the points I wouldn't budge on was finding my own passion and surprisingly, she was more than happy to help me find something that suited me.

"From escort, to marketing specialist—"

"*Back* to escort," Shae interrupted with a smirk.

"To interior designer," I said with a proud smile. Butterflies flew around my stomach and I couldn't help the sense of pride that swept over me.

I did end up dusting off that certificate and worked the last few years to get my name out there. I had to take more courses, apply for internships...but now I was finally able to call myself an interior designer.

"You don't want to miss your first day," she said. "I heard the boss is an asshole."

I rolled my eyes at her.

"You are kind of an asshole sometimes," I said.

Shae had, of course, tried to help me in her own way and that meant that she willingly started an entire company just so I—one day—could work there.

She had started it before I even told her what I was trying to do and it had gained some popularity after working on the houses of famous movie stars and influencers. Though I had a feeling she had still started it for me and me alone.

I embraced this part of her finally and reveled in the lengths she would go to for me. I only wished that one day, I could do the same for her.

"Do you think we can see the stars from here?" she asked and looked up to the darkening sky.

I sighed and leaned back into her, watching as the pinks and blues blended together above us.

"There is only one way to find out," I said and smiled at her. She leaned down to kiss me softly.

"I love you," she whispered.

Even now those words caused my heart to stop and my breath to catch.

"I love you too, Shae," I whispered.

Thanks for reading THE TIES THAT BIND US! Want more smutty sapphic romance? DON'T STOP ME is next in line and if you look carefully you may see a cameo from Shae and Jean in there as well!

From Eden Emory comes an f/f spicy dark age-gap romance between an adult club owner and her son's ex.

She was everything I ever wanted.

Smart. ***Beautiful.*** ***Passionate.***

I became obsessed with her, or at least who I thought she was.

And then, she showed me her **true colors,** by showing up on my doorstep as my son's girlfriend.

She was off-limits.

But I couldn't deny the part of me still wanted her and by the look in her eyes...

Neither could she.

Read Next

FOR NSFW T3BU art (and other series as seen above) join my Patreon!

There is also a few shorts and deleted scenes of the couple that you can take advantage of!

Check it out here or go to https://www.patreon.com/ellemae books

If you liked this, please review!

Reviews really help indie authors get their books out there so, please make sure to share your thoughts!

Want more smutty books?

Check out my pen name Elle Mae, for more paranormal spicy wlw books!

You can find me on instagram, Facebook, and tiktok @ellemaebooks

Check out my newest release here! Or search The Price of Silence: Winterfell Academy!

A snippet is included in this book!

Acknowledgments

Thank you to my loving partner for supporting me no matter the book.

And thank YOU the readers for going along with my late night ideas and supporting me no matter my path! Without you there would be no me! So thank you for making my author dreams come true!

About the Author

Eden Emory is a contemporary spicy pen name for Elle Mae. This pen name will mostly focus on spicy dark wlw romance that pushes the boundaries and incorporates troupes normally seen in f/m romance.

Eden Emory was born out of a want for more. More spice, more wlw, and even more smutty vibes with little to no plot.

Loved this book? Please leave a review!

For more behind the scene content, sign up for my newsletter at https://view.flodesk.com/pages/61722d0874d564fa09f4021b

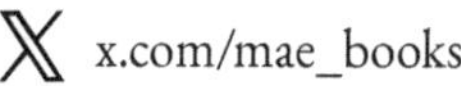

goodreads.com/ellemae